Christmas 1987

To Jeffrey,
Here's a book of some
interesting stories that
I'm sure will be some
of your favorite stories.
Merry Christmas!
Santa Claus

THE BEST FAIRY TALES

THE BROTHERS GRIMM

HANS CHRISTIAN ANDERSEN

THE BEST
FAIRY
TALES

THE
BROTHERS GRIMM

HANS
CHRISTIAN ANDERSEN

TREASURE PRESS

First published in Great Britain in 1984 by
Octopus Books Limited under the title
The Best Fairy Tales

This edition published in 1986 by
Treasure Press
59 Grosvenor Street
London W1

This edition © 1984 Octopus Books Limited

ISBN 1 85051 150 0

Printed in Yugoslavia by MK

— CONTENTS —

RED RIDING HOOD

Once upon a time there was a little girl who lived with her father and mother in a cottage on the edge of a big dark wood.

Everybody loved the dear little girl, and she was especially loved by her kind old Grandmamma who lived on the other side of the big wood in a cottage of her own.

When her Grandmamma was younger and was able to see well enough to make tiny neat stitches, she had sat down and cut out and sewn a beautiful cape and hood for her granddaughter. It was made out of a rich red velvet and it looked very handsome and cosy when it was finished.

The little girl could scarcely wait to try on the lovely cape and hood when it arrived. And when her mother had helped her to fasten it round her neck and tucked her ribbons under the hood, she had danced all round the kitchen in it.

From the moment of its arrival the little girl wore her red cape and hood as often as her mother would allow. She wore it about the house and in the garden, and she wore it to go to the village shops.

'Why, hello, little Red Riding Hood,' smiled the baker, when he saw her in it for the first time, and he gave her a biscuit covered with sticky sugar.

'Good-day to you, Red Riding Hood,' said the lady who sold sweets, when she saw her for the first time in her new outfit. And she gave her a handful of toffees.

'That's a fine bright red you're in today,' said the jolly fishmonger. And he gave her a little fish for her pussy cat who was waiting at home for her, before adding, 'You're a proper little Red Riding Hood you are!'

Soon everybody in the village was calling the little girl Red Riding Hood and if she had another name, which I'm sure she did, it was forgotten. Even her mother and her father called their golden-haired daughter Red Riding Hood.

Now although Red Riding Hood was old enough to go to the village shops all by herself and to help Mummy with all the dusting and the baking, she was not old enough to go into the dark woods.

This was mostly because of the big bad wolf who lived there. There were all kinds of scary stories about the big bad wolf which the boys in the village told each other in the evenings. And the very boldest of them would boast that they had seen the dreadful wolf among the trees as they walked in the woods.

Little Red Riding Hood knew about the fierce wolf, but she did not think about him much. She was such a gay, happy little girl that she found it hard to believe in witches or ogres or big bad wolves!

One morning, when Red Riding Hood was out in the garden pretending to chase the pretty butterflies, one of the huntsmen, a friend of her father's, came to the house. He had a message from Grandmamma. She had caught a very bad cold and was ill in bed and unable to do her shopping.

'Dear, oh, dear!' exclaimed little Red Riding Hood's mother. And she called her daughter in from the garden.

'Grandmamma is ill,' she told her. 'And I've promised to go into the village and help Mrs Brown today.'

'If you put some nice things in your shopping basket, I could take them to my Grandmamma,' said Red Riding Hood.

'That's a good idea,' said her mother with a sigh of relief. 'Now go and play in the garden again while I get the basket ready for you to take.'

So Red Riding Hood ran back into the garden and began her game again. But now there wasn't any fun in pretending to chase the butterflies. All she could think about was her poor Grandmamma lying ill in bed and perhaps needing her.

While little Red Riding Hood was in the garden, her mother took some delicious sugary doughnuts out of her tin and wrapped them up in some paper. Then she looked out a pot of honey and some fresh cream and a loaf of freshly baked bread and a slab of country butter.

There were so many things she found to put in the basket that she began to wonder whether little Red Riding Hood would be able to carry it.

When she was satisfied at last that she had packed the basket with everything Grandmamma might want, she covered its contents with a white cloth and called her daughter in from the garden.

While little Red Riding Hood was in the garden, her mother filled a basket with delicious food.

'Now remember,' she said, 'don't tip up the basket.'

'I'll remember,' the little girl said, as she put on her beautiful red cape. 'I'll hold it ever so carefully.'

'And give my fond love to Grand-mamma,' went on her mother as she walked with Red Riding Hood to the door. 'And tell her I'll be over tomorrow.'

'Yes, I'll do that,' Red Riding Hood said, taking the basket as they got outside.

'One thing more,' said her mother. 'Take the long way round. On no account must you go through the woods.'

'Of course not,' said the little girl.

She promised her mother that she would not go through the woods.

And away she went, taking the long dusty road that went all round the woods and ended up at her Grandmamma's cottage. What a lovely day it was! And oh how inviting the woods were with all the pretty flowers peeping through!

Once or twice Red Riding Hood found her feet taking her off the dusty old road and on to the grass.

It was so beautiful in the woods and such fun to be following the narrow woodland paths.

'It would save time,' she began to think. 'It would save lots of time if I took one of the short cuts through the woods. I wonder if I should?'

And before you could say Jack Robin, there she was, off the road, and into the pretty woods.

It was so beautiful in the woods, and such fun to be following the narrow woodland paths that Red Riding Hood did not give that big bad wolf a single thought. In fact she forgot all about him!

But he was there all right—and he was watching her! He licked his lips as he saw the little girl put down her basket and begin gathering some of the pretty flowers all about her. And at the sight of his fierce greedy look the scared little rabbits fled away to their burrows thankful that just for once the bad old wolf was not interested in them.

As for Red Riding Hood—well, she was thinking how the flowers would please her Grandmamma. So you can imagine what a surprise she got when the wolf at last made up his mind to show himself!

'Well, well, well,' said he, putting on a very mild and tame expression. 'What a pleasure to come across such a sweet child in the woods! Where are you going, my pretty? You can tell old wolfie.'

The wolf's voice was so friendly that Red Riding Hood, after her first start of fear, turned to him with a smile, 'I'm on my way to Grandmamma's cottage on the far side of these woods,' she said. 'These flowers are for her.'

'What a lucky old lady she must be,'

'I'm on my way to Grandmamma's cottage,' she said. 'These flowers are for her.'

said the wolf. 'Lives all alone, does she? On the other side of the wood you said? I must say I'd like somebody as pretty as you to visit me.'

'I've got all sorts of nice things in my basket for her,' said Red Riding Hood. 'I know she will be pleased to see me for she is not very well today.'

'Well, I won't delay you,' said the wolf. 'Goodbye my dear.'

And the wolf disappeared with a bound through the trees, leaving Red Riding Hood to finish gathering her flowers. If he was going to get to that cottage before her he would have to hurry.

Well, that big bad wolf was quite out of breath when Grandmamma's cottage

*The wolf disappeared,
leaving Red Riding Hood
to finish gathering her
flowers.*

17

came in sight, and he sat down for a moment to rest before going up to the door.

'Who is it?' came the old lady's feeble voice in answer to his knock.

'It's your own little Red Riding Hood,' replied the wolf. 'I have a lovely basket full of good things to eat.'

'I can't get up,' called out the old lady. 'Lift the latch and come in.'

The wolf lifted the latch. The door opened, and he was inside. Surely if he hadn't been such a dreadfully wicked old wolf the sight of the sweet little lady would have melted his heart. But he *was* a dreadfully wicked old wolf and so he ran to the bed and swallowed little Red Riding Hood's Grandmamma in one gulp.

Then he jumped into bed, put on her frilly white nightcap, tying its pink ribbon in a bow under his chin, and lay back comfortably to wait.

'I shall pretend to be the old lady,' the cunning wolf told himself. The child will be easily deceived. Pity she is so small— but she'll make a tasty morsel.'

The wolf lifted the latch of the door.

'Who is it?' came the old lady's feeble voice in answer to his knock.

19

'Lift the latch, child, and come straight in!'

In the meantime Red Riding Hood was drawing near to the cottage and she ran up the path and knocked at the door just as the wolf had done.

'Who is it?' the wolf called out.

'It's your very own little Red Riding Hood,' came the reply.

'Lift the latch, child,' the wolf said, 'and come straight in!' And he pulled down the white nightcap as far as it would go hoping to hide his ears, and he tightened the pink ribbon to hold it in place. Then he slipped under the bed-clothes so that they would hide his long whiskers and his cruel white teeth.

21

'I'm coming, Grandmamma,' the little girl shouted excitedly and, as the door sprang open, she skipped into the room.

'Come closer, come closer,' the wolf said in a hoarse whisper, as Red Riding Hood stood at the foot of the bed. 'Come closer and speak to your old Granny.'

'But—but Grandmamma,' said the girl, thinking her Grandmamma looked very, very strange. 'What big ears you have!'

'All the better to hear you with, my child,' came the reply.

'But Grandmamma, what big eyes you have!' said little Red Riding Hood.

'All the better to see you with, my dear!'

'But Grandmamma, what great big hands you have!' cried the little girl.

'All the better to hug you with,' came the reply.

And then, just for a moment, the wolf lifted his head and Red Riding Hood caught sight of his huge mouth and she called out, half in fear and half in surprise, 'Oh, Grandmamma, what a terrible big mouth you have!'

Now by this time the old wolf was in no doubt what he was going to do. He was going to leap out of bed and swallow the little girl in one gulp.

'Come closer child, do,' he said in a croaky whisper. 'Your old Granny wants to smell those pretty flowers you have picked in the woods.'

'You don't seem like my Grandmamma,' whispered Red Riding Hood. And instead of going up to the bed she turned away and put her basket down on the table.

The old wolf fumed with impatience as he said, 'Come, child, come closer.'

'But, Grandmamma,' the little girl said

22

'Come closer, come closer,' said the wolf.

*'But—but Grandmamma,
what big ears you have!*

in a whisper, 'You are so strange today
and you have such a terrible big mouth!'

'Oh-ho—all the better to eat you
with!' howled the wolf, as the little girl at
last came closer. And with a single bound
he leapt out of bed and there and then
gobbled her up.

Now that wicked, greedy old wolf had
had Grandmamma and little Red Riding
Hood for his dinner, so it was no wonder
that he began to feel very sleepy. He jumped back into bed, put his head on the pillow
and was soon fast asleep and snoring.

With a single bound he leapt out of bed.

His loud snores attracted the attention of a passing huntsman. 'Why the old lady must be ill if she is snoring so loudly, I'll just take a peep through her window to see if she is all right.'

His loud snores attracted the attention of a huntsman who was passing that way.

27

He raised his gun and shot the wolf dead.

Well, it didn't take him long to work out what had happened when he saw the old wolf. Raising his gun, he aimed at the wicked creature through the window, and shot him dead.

Then the huntsman, sad and sorry that he had arrived too late to save the old lady, put the wolf on the table and took out his big hunting scissors, thinking that he would have the wolf's skin.

Imagine his delighted surprise when, with the very first snip—out popped the old lady! And with his second snip—out came little Red Riding Hood!

'That was kind of you,' said little Red Riding Hood's Grandmamma. 'I didn't enjoy being inside that horrid creature a bit.'

'Nor me!' said little Red Riding Hood, and she reached up and gave the brave huntsman a big kiss.

Soon all three were sitting down to a

lovely tea of bread and honey and the sweet, sugary doughnuts which Red Riding Hood's mother had put in the basket. And after tea Grandmamma declared that she felt well enough to take care of herself for the rest of the day. So the huntsman and Red Riding Hood went off together through the woods, and there was no big bad wolf to scare the little girl on the way home!

Out popped the old lady and little Red Riding Hood!

THE UGLY DUCKLING

Once upon a time there was a handsome young duck who greatly looked forward to raising a new family. She made her nest among the reeds and grasses some distance away from the old farmhouse where she belonged.

It was summer and the fields were yellow with corn, the cattle were plump and the sky was nearly always blue. It was a splendid time to have a family, and the young mother-to-be was quite content to sit, day after day, on her precious eggs.

But long after the expected time of hatching, she was still there. And she grew somewhat bored with the long wait. Few visitors came to see her for her nest was well hidden both from the farmhouse and the road, and quite a long way from the duck-pond.

Those among her friends who knew she was about to become a mother were at first most attentive, but when the time passed for her eggs to hatch, they grew tired of coming to see her. It was so difficult to make conversation—so hard to think of something fresh to say at each visit.

So, in the end, they stopped coming altogether, and the poor duck got lonelier and lonelier.

'Will my babies never come?' she asked herself over and over again. 'How much longer must I sit here neglected by all my friends!'

But she was a faithful soul, and the thought of deserting her eggs never entered her head. On and on she sat, and the sun beat down on her head and made her even more uncomfortable and restless than she would have been if it hadn't shone at all.

She thought how delightful it would be to take a swim in the duck-pond or to spend the afternoon gossiping in the yard. But then she consoled herself with the thought of the pride she would have when at last she did become a mother.

Just when she was wondering if she could face another day of sitting, one of her eggs burst open. Then there was another tap-tap and a second shell broke.

Mother Duck—for now she had earned the title—was in raptures.

'At last, at last!' she told herself. 'I'm a mother at last!'

And she sat on with no hint of impatience, waiting for the rest of her eggs to crack.

Soon she had five chirping little babies, all active and healthy, and all

curious to know about the strange big world they now found themselves in.

'It only *seems* big and strange, my darlings,' said Mother Duck, who was still sitting on the last egg. 'It seems big because your other world, the one you have just left, was very small.'

Then she sighed, for the sight of her five lively children made her restless and she longed to be up and away with them. But how could she leave this last egg? Why was it so much bigger than the others and why, oh, why wouldn't it crack open?

Presently, one of the senior ducks in the yard came to pay her a visit and, after admiring the new chicks, she took a peek at the egg Mother Duck was sitting on.

'Bless my beak,' she cackled. 'I believe that's a turkey egg!'

'I don't believe it,' said Mother Duck firmly. 'It's true that it is very big and taking a long time to hatch but you'll see— out of it will come the finest baby of the lot!'

'I hope you're right,' said the old duck, 'I only hope you're right!'

Secretly alarmed, Mother Duck sat on. Just after her friend had departed, the great egg suddenly burst open and out came the ugliest little creature she had ever seen.

'That can't be one of mine!' she exclaimed, staring at it with open beak. 'Oh dear! Oh dear!'

Now the ugly little duckling wasn't really as ugly as poor Mother Duck fancied. It was only that he was quite different from his brothers and sisters. He

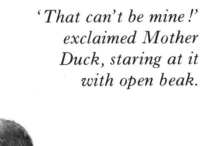

'That can't be mine!' exclaimed Mother Duck, staring at it with open beak.

was so strangely different that they began making fun of him almost as soon as he stepped out of the shell.

Mother Duck took her eyes away from her youngest and looked at the rest of her chicks. How pretty they were! How lively and full of fun! How proud she would be to show them off!

'Yes,' she decided, 'they are all just like their father—that is, all except one'... and she thought of what her old friend had said. But she concluded that it was quite impossible that she should have hatched a turkey egg. She had never heard of such a thing.

'I must make the best of him,' she told herself. 'He's mine, and the first thing I must do is to take him to the farmyard and show him off with the others. If his aunts and uncles approved of him, she had nothing to worry about.

She wished his father had been somewhere close, but truth to tell he had neglected her shamefully all the time she had been sitting on the eggs, and she was afraid he had lost interest in his new family. Anyway she would see . . .

So with a defiant 'Quack! Quack!' Mother Duck summoned her children and set out with them on the walk to the farm.

As she waddled along, her chicks strung out behind her like golden feather-

*Two naughty piglets came prancing up
and made some very unkind remarks
about the odd ugly duckling.*

ed balls on a chain—all except one, who
was a dull greyish colour—she wondered
and worried about the future of her
youngest.

The sun was warm. It was a splendid
day for a walk, and somehow or other by
the time Mother Duck had made her way
round the duck-pond and across the lane
that led to the farm she had forgotten most
of her worries.

Two of Mother Duck's sisters were
waiting for her, and as she paraded her
babies before them one of them fixed her
eyes on the little ugly duckling.

'Goodness gracious me!' she quacked.

'That's not one of yours, surely?'

'He most certainly is!' replied the
Mother Duck. 'I admit he's not quite the
same as his brothers and sisters, but he is
mine and—and I'm proud of him.' She
said this because she was a true mother.

Just then two naughty piglets came
prancing up and made some very unkind
remarks about the odd ugly duckling,
which caused his little brothers to snigger
spitefully.

Poor Mother Duck! She wanted to
love all her children equally but there was
still the doubt in her mind that the grey
duckling might not be a duckling at all.

*'That's not one of
yours, surely?'
asked one of
Mother Duck's
friends.*

So, when the moment was right, she made off, calling the ducklings to follow her. 'We are all going for a swim,' she said, knowing that if her ugly duckling did happen to be a turkey chick he would not be able to swim!

Her five babies jumped into the water and began swimming as if they hadn't a care in the world, and the ugly duckling swam with them, and he was just as much at home in the water as his brothers and sisters!

Mother Duck was delighted. She knew now, without a shadow of a doubt, that her youngest was not a turkey child, because turkeys cannot swim.

Back she went to the farmyard to introduce her family to the oldest and most respected duck there—the Grand Duchess of the poultry-farm—who had to approve every new-born chick.

'Shake yourselves, don't turn your

'We don't want you here!' hissed one of the older ducks. 'Get out!'

toes in!' Mother Duck whispered to her brood as they prepared for the inspection. 'I do so want you to make a good impression.'

Alas, the ugly duckling did not pass the inspection. The Grand Duchess announced that he was, unlike the others, a complete failure, and she gave him a very nasty nip—for she was a spiteful old lady when anything displeased her.

Mother Duck was most bitterly disappointed and ashamed. She was not even comforted when the Grand Duchess said, 'Your other children are pretty enough, but I cannot say anything good about your youngest. It seems to me that he does not belong here at all. In fact his appearance quite offends me!'

To be condemned in public by the Grand Duchess was the most dreadful thing that could happen to any member of the poultry-yard.

Mother Duck hung her head and wished she had never been born, and the poor little grey duckling who had fluffed out his feathers and remembered not to turn his toes in could not understand why he had failed to pass the test.

He, too, felt terribly ashamed, and he wished he could find a place to hide until all the fuss was over.

But worse was to follow. Now that the Grand Duchess had condemned him, he became the target for all the other birds, and not even his mother dared to come to his rescue.

His aunts and uncles turned their backs on him, and some very bad-tempered hens chased him all over the yard.

How frightened he was as he tried to dodge their cruel pecks.

'We don't want you here,' one of them hissed. 'You will bring disgrace to the whole poultry family here. Get out! Get out!'

That first week was a terrible one for the poor duckling. Wherever he went he was attacked. Even his brothers and sisters, who might have been expected to have some love for him, teased him and made fun of him.

'You're not one of us,' they told him. 'You're clumsy and ugly and we're ashamed of you—even our mother is ashamed of you—so why don't you go away and leave us in peace?'

The poor duckling did his best to defend himself but he was no match for his brothers and sisters or the fierce hens, who seem to have taken a particular dislike to him.

At last he could stand it no longer. He made up his mind to run away. He chose a time when it was growing dark, and he ran and flew over the fence and found himself almost at once on a great moor where the wild ducks lived. Here he lay all night long, miserable and afraid.

Early the next morning the handsome wild ducks invited the little duckling to join him in their stretch of water.

But soon they, too, began to make fun

He was no match for the fierce hens, who seemed to have taken a particular dislike to him.

of him. 'Who *are* you?' one asked. 'I've never before set eyes on such a strange little monster!'

The duckling did his best to pretend he had not heard. He tried to make himself as pleasant as possible, and asked if he might stay with the wild ducks.

'You can stay if you like,' they told him in a haughty way, 'so long as you don't imagine you are good enough to marry into our family.'

He tried to make himself as pleasant as possible, and asked if he could stay with the wild ducks.

At this the big drake, who had joined their company, looked most superior and shook his head at the poor duckling.

Then the wild ducks all flew away and as they rose from the water, there was a loud bang and two fell dead in the swamp.

Terrified, the ugly duckling hid among the reeds until a great dog came sniffing round him. He almost died with fright, but the dog did not harm him. Instead it went on into the swamp and picked up one of the dead ducks in its big mouth.

Trembling, the ugly duckling kept his eyes on the fierce dog and saw that it carried the handsome dead duck to a man with a gun and laid it at his feet. The man with the gun was not satisfied with just one duck, and he raised his gun again.

Bang! Bang! Another of the ducks, which had so recently been talking to the ugly duckling, fell out of the air.

'How awful!' the little duckling thought, as he flattened himself out among the reeds. 'That might have been me! This is a terrible place. I can't stay here.'

But he waited a long time before he dared to cross the moor. All that day he walked until, at last, he came to a little hut.

The ugly duckling almost died with fright, but the great dog did not harm him.

It was a miserable little hut, but the ugly duckling thought it might give him some shelter for the night, and he slipped in through one of the wide cracks in the door.

It was a miserable little hut, with an old battered door and holes in the roof, but the ugly duckling thought that it might give him some shelter for the night, and he slipped in through one of the wide cracks in the door.

How thankful the little duckling was to have found a place to shelter in! But the hut was not empty; in it lived an old woman with her cat and her hen.

The cat was called Sonnie and whenever she spoke to it, it arched its back and purred. It could even give out sparks. The hen was called Chickabiddy-Shortshanks and it had very short legs.

The woman loved them both but she loved the hen better than the cat because it laid her beautiful fresh eggs for her breakfast.

The duckling crept into a dark corner and was not immediately noticed, and he closed his eyes and thought of the haughty ducks who had called him a monster, and the fierce dog who had ignored him.

'Perhaps,' he thought, 'I was too ugly even for that dog to touch me! It's quite possible!' And he sighed and wished, not for the first time, that he had never been born.

Presently, the old woman lit a candle and placed it on the table and its flickering light showed her quite plainly that she had a visitor. She looked at the quivering grey duckling in his corner and she said, 'What's this?'

But she could not see very well and she thought the duckling was a fat duck who had strayed into her hut from one of the farms.

Sonnie the cat purred, and Chickabiddy-Shortshanks cackled loudly at the sound of their mistress's voice, and the old woman smiled.

'They like you,' she told the frightened duckling. 'That's for certain. And I like you too, for now I shall have duck's eggs for my supper.'

So the little duckling was made welcome in the hut, and the woman said that she would give him three weeks' trial, and that during all that time she would feed him twice a day.

The next morning the duckling became acquainted with the cat and the hen.

The cat told him that it was the master of the house and should be obeyed in all things. And the hen told him that it knew everything that was going on in the world and should never, never be contradicted.

The ugly duckling told them about the poultry-yard, and the moor and the fierce dog, but the cat soon grew tired of listening and the hen said that his story was very boring.

'Can you lay eggs?' it asked suddenly.

And the duckling said, 'No! Is that important?'

'It's *very* important,' said the hen. 'You'll soon find out for yourself . . .'

'Can you purr and arch your back?' asked the cat.

And the duckling said, 'No! Is that important?'

'It's *very* important,' said the cat. 'You are nothing if you can't purr and arch your back. I suppose you can't make sparks come out of your feathers?'

'No, I can't,' confessed the duckling miserably. 'I can't make sparks.'

'I thought not,' said the cat. 'Your opinion is of no interest to us because you can do none of the things that make you respected.'

Then they went to the old woman and told her that the duckling was quite useless.

'Ah,' said the old woman, who still believed that the duckling was a nice fat duck, 'but I know she isn't quite useless; she is soon going to lay me a lovely fresh egg for my supper.'

The ugly duckling looked up at the old woman and thought she had a kind face. But he kept silent because he was not sure what she would do if he told her that he could not lay eggs, and he was grateful to the hen for keeping silent on that matter.

That morning the duckling told the hen all about swimming and diving, and how wonderful he felt when he was in the water.

'I have no use for water at all,' said the hen, 'except of course to drink. And as far as I know Sonnie feels just the same about it. Sonnie hates getting wet and so, too, does our mistress. And there's no one wiser than the old lady, I assure you.'

The ugly duckling was disappointed. He had been sure the hen and the cat would feel the same way as he did about diving and swimming. It seemed he didn't have anything in common with them.

But the old lady kept on feeding him and he had the shelter of the hut at night so he kept quiet.

After a few days, the woman said to him, 'Have you laid me an egg?'

And the ugly duckling shook his head, feeling quite ashamed.

'Ah well,' said she, 'there is time yet.'

But after a week the duckling had still not laid an egg, and the old woman was growing angry and impatient. She spoke

The ugly duckling looked up at the old woman and thought she had a kind face.

sharply to the duckling, and the cat and hen, taking their cue from their mistress, began telling him that he was nothing but a lazy good-for-nothing, and not earning his keep.

'If you don't lay eggs,' said the cat, 'you've no business to be here,' and it hissed and showed its claws.

The hen gave him a vindictive peck, and the old woman smiled and said it was really no more than such an ugly, useless creature deserved.

Miserable and unhappy, the ugly duckling decided that he could no longer stay in the hut.

'It's time,' he told himself, 'for me to go out into the world again.' And he sought out the cat and said, 'I'm going away.'

'You do that,' answered the cat. 'Nobody wants you here.'

The beautiful birds were dazzlingly white with long graceful necks, and the ugly duckling looked up at them, full of admiration and envy. If only he could be like them!

So the ugly duckling left the hut. He walked a long way until he came to a small pond. His spirits rose at the sight of the water and he dived right in.

How happy he was to find himself swimming and diving again. He longed to make friends with the little birds and the wild creatures who came to drink there, but none of them seemed to want to have anything to do with him. And the duckling told himself for the hundredth time that it was because he was so ugly.

One day, towards the end of summer, some beautiful birds flew overhead. They were dazzlingly white with long graceful necks and the ugly duckling looked up at them, full of admiration and envy. If only he could be like them!

Soon, however, he forgot about the beautiful birds. Autumn had come; the wind was cold and all the little birds flew away. Then came winter. It grew colder and colder. Ice formed on the water and the duckling had to swim up and down to prevent the ice from trapping him. When he was too tired to swim any more, he became a prisoner of the cruel ice, and would have perished if a farmer had not seen his plight.

The farmer broke the ice with his big heavy boots and picked up the duckling and took him home.

Then came the winter and the weather grew colder and colder.

Ice formed on the water and the little duckling had to swim up and down to prevent the cruel ice from trapping him.

The farmer's children wanted to play with the duckling, and the boy tried to catch him as he flew around the kitchen. Terrified, the little duckling upset the milk-pan, and then flew into the butter-tub, and the farmer's wife screamed at him and began chasing him all over the kitchen while the children laughed and

The boy tried to catch him as he flew around the kitchen. Terrified, the little duckling managed to make for the open door and fly out into the fields.

shrieked for joy. They did not mean to be cruel but the poor ugly duckling thought his last hour had come; using up all his strength, he managed to make for the open door and fly out into the fields, where he lay, hidden by some bushes, on the hard-frozen snow.

What a terrible time for him now followed! He was buffetted by the icy winds and almost frozen to death. But somehow or other he managed to make his way to a lonely stretch of moorland where he found shelter until the worst of the winter had passed.

He had very little to eat and was so weak from hunger that for long days at a time he stayed in one spot, his eyes closed.

How he managed to survive that long

dreary winter he would never know! When it was over at last, and the first hint of spring was in the air, the ugly duckling was suddenly aware that all around him the moors and the forests were coming alive again.

Larks sang in the sky. Squirrels chattered in the trees. There were rabbits and other small creatures to be seen everywhere.

Now he no longer felt so alone, and he took heart and began to wonder where he could go next.

He found that he could flap his wings. They beat the air so strongly that it was easy for him to fly and, with a cry of joy, he rose into the sky. He flew over the moors and the forests until he came to a beautiful garden with trees and shrubs.

He had very little to eat and was so weak from hunger that for long days at a time he stayed in one spot.

He found that he could flap his wings. They beat the air so strongly that it was easy for him to fly.

In the centre of this garden was a lake and, at the sight of the vast expanse of water, the ugly duckling knew that he would be happy swimming there. Then he noticed the graceful long-necked birds that he had seen once before.

Oh, how graceful they were! How he longed to join them as they swam up and down on the lake. Such beautiful birds would never, never be friends with

How he longed to join the graceful long-necked birds as they swam up and down on the lake.

The swans began to
circle around him
and, not daring to
lift his eyes, the
duckling stared into
the water.

52

him, of that he was certain. And so the duckling flew down to the very edge of the lake and stood there, eyeing them enviously. They paid no attention to him and he thought, 'It's not very surprising that they should ignore me! They consider me too ugly to speak to.'

As he watched the royal birds, the duckling began to tremble he was so anxious to speak to them. 'Even if they kill me,' he told himself at last, 'I'll make myself known to them.'

And he flew out into the water and swam towards the graceful swans. They saw him coming and they began gliding towards him.

'Kill me!' cried the brave duckling. 'I don't deserve to live. Everywhere I go I'm hated because I'm so ugly.'

And he bent his head, feeling sure that the beautiful birds would attack him and drive him away.

This did not happen. The swans began to circle around him and, not daring to lift his eyes, the duckling stared into the water. The water was so clear that it was like a mirror, and the duckling saw himself reflected on the surface.

As he stared at his reflection, he saw that he, too, had the long slender neck and gorgeous plumage of the birds he so admired. Scarcely able to believe what he saw, he raised his head.

'Welcome, brother,' said the other swans. 'We're happy that you have come to live among us. Stay with us. Make this lake your home.'

Presently some children came to the edge of the lake. They began throwing bread to the swans, and the voice of one of the boys rang out across the water.

'Look! Look! A new swan! He is the youngest and the most handsome of all the swans. He must be their king!'

The new swan did not feel like a king. But, oh, how happy he was! He was happier than he had ever dreamed was possible when he was an ugly duckling. Now, at last, he had found his true home!

THE EMPEROR'S NEW CLOTHES

Once upon a time, a very long time ago, there lived an Emperor who loved to wear new clothes. Every spare wardrobe in his palace was packed from ceiling to floor with gorgeous waistcoats, tunics and capes.

The palace carpenters spent much of their time putting up new shelves to hold the thousands of pairs of shoes which the Emperor was always buying. There were red shoes, and blue shoes and yellow shoes and brown shoes. And some had gold buckles and some silver and many had bows.

Then there were his hats—all very splendid and gorgeous and most of them decked out with curling feathers and large buckles. Some of these hats the Emperor wore only once for he loved best to wear something which was absolutely and entirely new. In fact the Emperor was so fond of new clothes that he would declare a hat or a cape or a tunic out of fashion if he had been seen wearing it more than twice in one week!

If you said that this Emperor had a passion for new clothes you would be quite right. Everybody knew about it. His own people had to pay high taxes so that their Emperor would have enough gold to spend on the silks, and brocades and rich velvets which were sent to him from other countries. And the richest men in the Emperor's empire were those who could design something new in the way of breeches or fancy shirts or gorgeous frilly collars and cravats.

Sad to say, the Emperor did not pay much attention to important matters like building new ships or making friends with other countries. He was usually too busy with his new clothes to have time for the Ambassadors and the Foreign Ministers who came to see him. And if anyone wished to find the Emperor in a hurry he would visit the mirrors first.

The Emperor was very fond of his mirrors. He had a vast number of them—all over the palace—and he had an army of Mirror-Polishers who spent all their days just cleaning and polishing the Emperor's mirrors.

Now the Emperor's love for new clothes and his delight in new and beautiful materials brought a great many merchants to the court.

'We must see the Emperor,' they would say. 'We want to show him a roll of rich blue velvet or a dazzling length of brocade which he will simply adore.'

Sometimes the Emperor was pleased with the merchants and sometimes he was not, but he never failed to see them in case he should miss a bargain.

One day two strangers came to the city. One was round and fat and jolly and the other tall and thin with a long, serious face.

'I expect they want to see the Emperor,' said one of the women at the fountain, as they watched them. 'They look like weavers.'

Presently the two strangers began asking the way to the Emperor's palace, saying that they had something to tell the Emperor which would please him greatly.

Now the two weavers were really and truly villains, but very clever ones and as they made their way to the palace, they talked of their plans.

'It will be easy to persuade that vain and foolish Emperor to listen to us,' said the thin rogue.

'Especially when we tell him that we

The Emperor was usually to be found in front of a mirror, admiring his latest suit of clothes.

One day two strangers came to the city.

can weave the finest cloth any one has ever seen,' said the fat one. 'He won't be able to refuse our request.' And he gave a delighted chuckle.

'We shall have to be very serious,' warned his friend, as the palace came in sight. 'First we must persuade the Emperor to let us set up a loom in his palace.'

'Then we must tell him that to obtain the services of two such skilled weavers he must pay out much gold!' laughed the

The weavers set up their loom in the Emperor's palace.

fat villain, who had the annoying habit of laughing at everything he said.

'Leave the talking to me,' said his companion. 'You'll see, we shall be given a room in the palace and setting up our loom in no time at all.'

He was right! When the Emperor heard that the weavers could weave the most wonderful stuff in the world, he gave them a bag of gold and told them to begin work at once.

'Just before we begin,' said the thin weaver in a humble voice, 'we must warn Your High and Mighty Majesty that our cloth has a wonderful quality. It is not visible to anyone who is stupid or unfit to hold an important office . . .'

'I understand,' said the Emperor. 'Only those who are clever and who are worthy to be important ministers will see it!'

Soon everybody in the market-place was talking about the two clever weavers and the marvellous cloth they were busy weaving for the Emperor's pleasure.

'It must be wonderful,' said one of the women. 'I hear they demand gold every day so that they can buy silks . . .'

Everybody in the market-place talked about the weavers and the marvellous cloth they were weaving.

Meantime, as the two false weavers pretended to work, they sent reports to the Emperor of the wonderful patterns they were weaving. The Emperor, of course, was filled with longing to inspect their loom and see for himself how the cloth was growing.

'I will go myself,' he thought. 'And see how much they have done.' Then he

'The colours are magnificent, Your Majesty!' whispered the minister.

had a second thought. 'Supposing I can't see this wonderful material. It is just possible that I am not clever enough or wise enough . . .'

He didn't really believe this, being a vain and conceited fellow, but in the end he decided to send his oldest and most trusted minister.

Away went the old man to the room where the weavers sat at their loom. And, lo and behold, the minister could see nothing. How foolish he felt and how fearful! If he told the Emperor that he could

The Emperor gave the weavers several bags of gold.

not see the cloth, then he would surely be dismissed from his important office. Shaking all over, he returned to the Emperor and told him that the cloth was so beautiful that he could not find words to describe it.

'The colours are magnificent, Your Majesty,' he whispered, 'and the patterns quite unusual and beautiful.'

Delighted with his minister's report, the Emperor sent for the two rogues and gave them several more bags of gold, telling them to work hard.

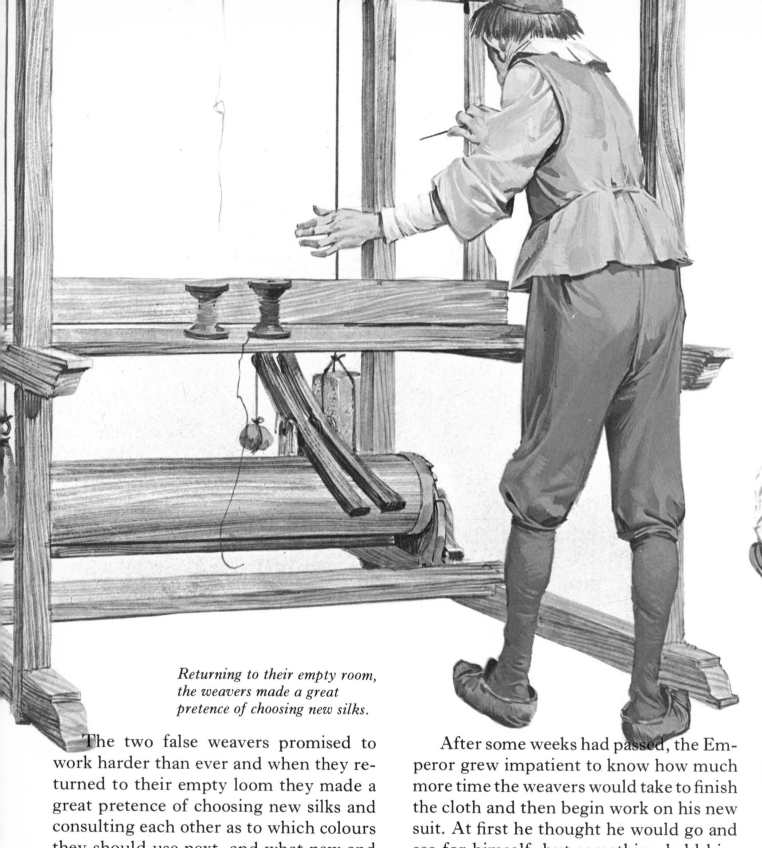

Returning to their empty room, the weavers made a great pretence of choosing new silks.

The two false weavers promised to work harder than ever and when they returned to their empty loom they made a great pretence of choosing new silks and consulting each other as to which colours they should use next, and what new and dazzling patterns they should introduce.

Meantime, quite a number of the lords and ladies of the court had come to inspect the weavers' work. They saw nothing but, of course, did not dare admit this.

After some weeks had passed, the Emperor grew impatient to know how much more time the weavers would take to finish the cloth and then begin work on his new suit. At first he thought he would go and see for himself, but something held him back and he sent for his Master of Wardrobes, a very honest man.

'Go to the weavers,' he told his Master of Wardrobes, 'and ask them to show you what they have done. Then report back to

'I shall depend upon you for a good report of the cloth,' the Emperor told his Master of Wardrobes.

me. I shall depend on you for a good description of the cloth.'

As he spoke, one of the rogues came into the throne room to ask for another fresh load of silks, and the Emperor willingly gave him a great number of silken reels of many brilliant colours.

'I am quite fond of blue,' said he, as the Master of the Wardrobes hurried away. 'Make certain you use plenty of that colour.'

And with a cunning smile on his round fat face the weaver agreed as he bowed himself out of the Emperor's presence.

Now the two rogues had taken lodgings in a part of the town which was quite a long way from the palace and, later that day, the Master of Wardrobes set out to visit their lodging-house for he had heard that the weavers did not work at their frames in the afternoon.

'The Emperor commands that you take me to your loom,' said he, as one of the rogues came to the door. 'I want to see for myself what progress you are making.'

'I'll be glad to,' said the rogue, who had been busy filling his travel-bags with the rich silks and the gold thread. 'Just wait here and I'll be with you in a moment. I can assure you that you are in for a very pleasant surprise.'

Both weavers accompanied the Master of Wardrobes back to the palace and, on the way, they talked with enthusiasm of their work.

'The colours will dazzle your eyes,' said one.

'The enchanting patterns will fill you with wonder,' said the other. 'You will find it hard to describe them to the Emperor.'

'I shall do what I can to give a true description to my Lord,' said the Master of Wardrobes with dignity, as they entered the room where the weavers had set up their loom.

'Well, here we are!' cried the thin weaver. 'Look, is the cloth not quite gorgeous? Is it not everything we said it was?'

'The Emperor commands that you take me to your loom,' said he, as one of the rogues came to the door.

'Look at the colours!' exclaimed the second weaver. 'Have you ever seen such brilliant blues?'

'Look at the colours!' exclaimed the second weaver. 'Have you ever seen such brilliant blues? And the patterns—are they not superb?'

The Master of Wardrobes stared at the empty loom. Then he rubbed his eyes and looked again. He could see nothing. The frames, his eyes told him, were empty. But then he knew, as everybody knew, that only those who were worthy of high positions at court would be able to see the wonderful cloth. Clearly he was not worthy. That was why he could see nothing of the cloth! But how could he admit this? No, no, he must pretend. So, he stood there, and the longer he stood

'The patterns woven in the cloth are most artistic!' he told the Emperor.

the easier it was to utter words like, *Magnificent! Splendid*, and *Quite Wonderful!*

Then he left the weavers and returned to the Emperor to make his report.

'Tell me, my good Master of all my Wardrobes,' the Emperor began. 'What is your opinion of the weavers' work?'

'Masterly! Wonderful!' exclaimed the poor courtier. 'Never have I seen such colours, and the patterns woven into the cloth are most artistic!'

'Ah!' exclaimed the Emperor, very pleased. 'I can well believe what you say. And I am looking forward to the time when I shall see this wonderful cloth for myself. I know I shall not be disappointed by the material.'

The Master of Wardrobes bowed, and blushed. He was, by nature, an honest man and it was difficult for him to tell his Emperor such a huge lie.

'Would it not be wise,' he suggested at

last, 'to send the Master Tailor to view the cloth? After you have received his report you will be able to start thinking about the kind of suit you desire.'

'That is an excellent idea!' said the Emperor. And he dismissed the Master of the Wardrobes there and then, and summoned his Master Tailor, who came, hat in hand and eager to please.

'Go at once to the weavers,' ordered his Emperor, 'and inspect the cloth they are weaving for me. I would like you to tell me what kind of suit it will make.'

'Certainly, certainly,' said the Tailor. 'I will go at once.'

'Go at once to the weavers,' ordered the Emperor, 'and inspect the cloth they are weaving for me.'

The weavers were seemingly hard at work when the Master Tailor entered the room, and they greeted him eagerly.

'We are thinking of using more blue silk for this length of cloth,' cried the thin-faced rogue. 'But naturally we shall value your opinion.'

The Master Tailor stepped up to the empty frames. He examined them closely as if deep in thought. Of course he could not see anything, but he was too cunning to say so. He knew very well that this must be because he was not quite worthy of his high office.

He hummed a little tune under his breath to show the weavers that he was completely at his ease. Then he said that they must not expect him to give an opinion all at once.

'Give me a moment to consider the silks,' he said. 'Yes, yes, I think you should use a trifle more of the blue. It is one of our Emperor's favourite colours.'

And he continued to stare at the empty frames as if he were admiring the design and the richness of the cloth.

'A very excellent idea!' cried the thin weaver. 'We shall introduce more of the blue silk and perhaps more gold thread.'

When the Master Tailor had given the two weavers some ten minutes of his valuable time, he took his departure. But, oh dear, how miserable and depressed he was as he left them for now he must find something to say to his Emperor.

'Am I smart enough to make him believe I have really seen the gorgeous material?' he asked himself. 'Oh well, I can always say what a fine suit it will make. And perhaps suggest that he has the new hat trimmed with the same wonderful material.'

He stared at the empty frames as if he were admiring the design and richness of the cloth.

The Emperor was not in the throne room but outside in the courtyard, having just returned from a ride in his coach.

'You will be highly delighted with the cloth,' the Master Tailor said, going up to him. 'It is quite remarkable, I do assure you, and I took the liberty to tell the weavers to use more of the blue silk. Such an attractive shade of blue it is—and your favourite colour . . .'

The Master Tailor broke off for he was now at a loss for words. The Emperor,

however, was smiling in a pleased fashion.

'Do you know,' he said at last, 'I have a mind to visit these two splendid fellows myself. I have had so many fine reports of their work from my ministers that I am now confident I shall not be in any way disappointed.'

'Then I will conduct you to their room,' cried the Master Tailor, greatly relieved. 'You will then see for yourself how very beautiful the cloth has turned out to be.' And he led the way back into

'*You will be highly delighted with the cloth,*' *the Master Tailor told the Emperor.*

70

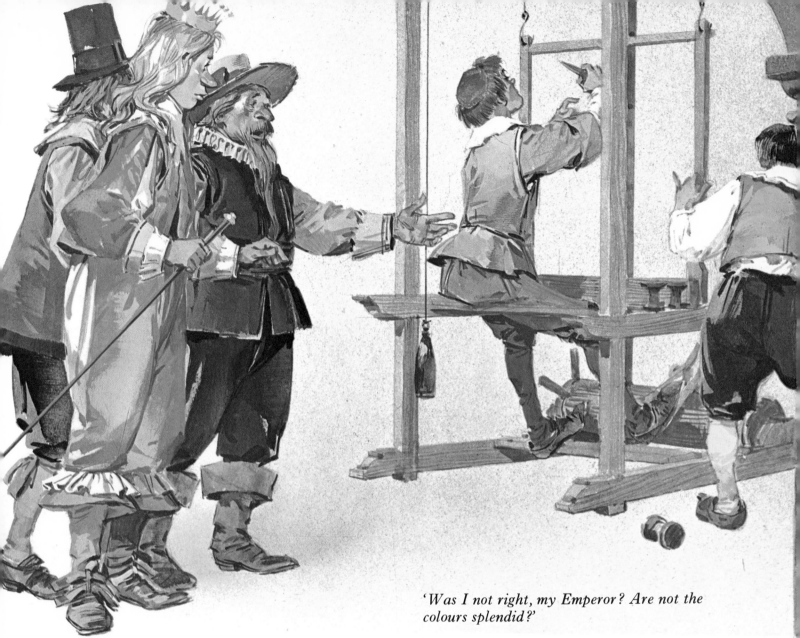

'Was I not right, my Emperor? Are not the colours splendid?'

the palace, happy in the knowledge that the Emperor had no reason to doubt his word or to suspect that anything was wrong.

Now the two rogues, who had very sharp ears, heard the approach of the royal party a long way off. This gave them plenty of time to take up their positions at the loom. In fact they did not turn round when the Emperor and his ministers came into their work-room. Instead, they pretended to be completely taken up with what they were doing—which was nothing at all!

As for the poor Emperor! The merry smile disappeared from his face as he gazed at the loom. Was there something dreadfully wrong with his eyes?

As he stared at the empty loom, the Master Tailor, thinking that he must say a few words in praise of the weavers, began to exclaim in a loud voice, 'Was I not right, my Emperor? Are not the colours splendid and the patterns unusual?'

For a moment the Emperor was too upset to speak. Then he said in his most lofty and important voice, 'Yes, yes, the cloth is quite superb. I am well pleased with it.'

And he blinked and nodded his head

71

Smiling and bowing, the weavers asked for more gold.

as he asked himself if, after all, he had spent too much time on his new clothes instead of the affairs of state and was, therefore, quite useless as an Emperor.

So overcome was he at this thought that he said he must take some fresh air, and the two weavers followed him outside into the courtyard, smiling and bowing, and at the same time asking for more gold.

'Certainly, certainly,' said the Emperor. 'Now tell me, my good men, when will you be ready to begin cutting out?'

'Almost at once, sire,' said one.

'We hope to begin this very day,' said the other, with another low bow, and a broad smile on his round, fat face.

And that very afternoon the two false weavers brought out their scissors and their chalk and their measuring rule and set to work. At least they pretended to work as they moved about their workroom or sat at their long work-bench, scissors in hand. And there was no one, not a single visitor who came to watch them, dared to say that they could not see anything of the grand cloth.

The two villains were much too clever to hurry when it came to the all important matter of cutting out a suit for the High and Mighty Emperor.

They made their game of pretence last for one whole week. Then, at the end

They brought scissors and chalk and set to work.

of the seven days, they went to the Emperor to inform him that they were now ready to give him his first fitting.

'We have brought the unfinished suit to show you, sire,' said one of the weavers. 'You can see for yourself how splendid it looks although there is still much to do.'

The poor Emperor managed a smile as the fat weaver held out his arms. He could not see anything, but he knew that others,

those worthy of their high positions at Court, were able to see and praise the work of the two weavers. Whatever happened none of his courtiers must guess that he saw nothing—not even a single strand of the expensive blue silk woven into the cloth!

'The suit is splendid,' he said warmly. 'Come to my rooms this afternoon and I will allow you to give me a fitting.'

'We have brought the unfinished suit to show you, sire.'

The Emperor stood patient and smiling while they tried on the invisible waistcoat and the breeches.

Well satisfied with their interview, the rogues departed, carrying the invisible suit as if it were the most fragile and precious thing on earth.

As for the Emperor he spent an anxious hour waiting for the weavers and when they came he stood patient and smiling while they tried on the invisible waistcoat and the breeches.

'How does it feel, sire?' asked one.

'We could take in the breeches just a trifle,' said the other.

'Just a trifle then,' said the Emperor, smiling and smiling.

The weavers promised that they would return the gorgeous suit in time for the Grand Procession. All the people would be lining the streets to watch their great Emperor parade in his wonderful new

clothes. And the two rogues came back to the palace quite quickly. But they refused to take part in the procession. Instead they ran back to their lodgings, where their bags were already stuffed with gold and silver, and silk thread, and then hurried away from the town as fast as their legs would take them.

What a strange, comic sight the foolish Emperor made as he set off down the street! But not one of his humble subjects dared even to smile—not even when one of the solemn attendants pretended to trip over the Emperor's train!

Then, all at once, a little boy cried out, 'Look, Daddy! Do look! Our mighty Emperor isn't wearing any . . .'

'Hush, child,' his father whispered, but already those around him were beginning to smile and then chuckle, and their mirth swelled into a roar of loud laughter.

In a sudden blinding flash the vain Emperor saw how he had been tricked and cheated. But being a mighty Emperor, with purple blood in his veins, he held his head all the higher and walked on and on down that long street.

'Look! Do look! Our mighty Emperor isn't wearing any . . .'

THE LITTLE MATCH GIRL

There was once upon a time a little girl who had no shoes to wear—not even in the winter time. This little girl was perhaps eight years old and she lived in the very poorest part of a big town.

If she had a proper name of her own, no one knew it. She was known everywhere as the little match girl, because each day she went out into the streets to sell bundles of matches.

In the summer the little match girl did not mind that she had no shoes. The sun warmed her bare feet as she went among the shoppers or talked to some of the friends she had made.

There was the pretty young flower-girl who sold tiny bunches of violets to the passing gentlemen, and the street bird-seller with his birds in a large cage. And the watercress girl who always greeted her with a friendly smile.

But in the winter the flower-girl and the watercress girl were no longer to be found, and the little match girl was sure then that she did not have a friend in the world.

Once she did have someone very close to her who had loved her—her grandmother. But the old lady had died and the match girl had only the memory of her grandmother's love to comfort her.

One year the snows came much earlier than usual. And by Christmas the pavements were slippery with ice, and the cruel wind had whipped the snow into deep drifts against the walls and the shop fronts.

The rich men of the town wore their warmest coats and mufflers and their tall hats to protect them against the biting wind. They were so anxious to be back in their cosy houses that they paid no attention to the little match girl. And they certainly did not think of buying any matches from her.

It is true it was a jolly time of year, but their minds were full of thoughts about the presents they must find for their families, and all the food they would presently be enjoying.

So the little girl sold very few of her bundles of matches over Christmas, and on New Year's Eve her father sent her out again. He was a hard, cruel man with no thought for his child. Even her mother did not pretend to love the little girl, or seem to care that she wore only a thin cotton blouse and patched skirt.

Their attic, its cracks stuffed with straw, was such a miserable place to live that the woman had long ago given up trying to be cheerful or to make those about her happy. She thought only of the money the little girl would give her at the end of the day.

'You can put my old slippers on your feet,' the mother told her daughter, as she gave her the matches. 'And mind you do better than you did yesterday.'

Shivering with cold, the little match girl crept out into the streets. But the slippers were much too big for her small feet, and soon one had fallen off, and a ragged boy snatched it and ran away with it.

Then the other slipper came off and

The rich people of the town were anxious to be back in their cosy houses.

was lost in the snow and the little girl wandered on through the streets, her toes blue with cold.

How she envied the well-dressed ladies of the town with their fur bonnets and fur muffs. How she wished that some of these rich ladies would notice her and out of the kindness of their hearts offer to buy some of her matches.

She waited by the coach and thought sadly that even the old horse had a better coat then she had.

Some of the men carried packages under their arms, for it was still the season of good will and present-giving.

The little match girl had never had a present in her life except a tiny bunch of spring flowers from the flower-girl and that was long ago. And as she stood there hoping she would be noticed, she began to wonder what might be in some of the

They paid no attention to the little match girl shivering with cold.

parcels. Perhaps the gentleman in the blue coat was taking a doll home to his granddaughter or a cuddly bear!

She thought she could guess what was in the bottle the big tall man with the red nose was carrying and, as he passed her, she called out hopefully, 'Buy some matches, sir? Please take some!'

But the big tall man did not even turn his head to look her way, and the little girl sighed, wondering whether her father would beat her if she did not make any money that day.

The snow was falling now so thickly that her hair and face were powdered with it, and she was so cold that she could not stop shivering. Yet she dared not go home. If she did, there would be no one to give her a kind word and more than likely her father would turn her out again. And when she thought of home she remembered only the wind whistling through the gaps in the roof and the bare wooden floor and the straw bed upon which she had to lie.

'No, I will not go home,' the little girl told herself bravely. 'Surely some kind lady or gentleman will buy some of my matches before the day is out!'

And she began walking up and down the long street and sometimes approaching one or two of the jollier looking ladies with a shy request that they take home some of her matches.

Sadly, although the ladies and their husbands had only moments before been busy wishing each other happiness for the New Year, they did not think of the girl's happiness or what it would mean to her if they gave her a little money.

When she spoke to them, they looked the other way or buried their faces deep in their high collars or mufflers and hurried on.

Now the little girl was so numb with cold that she felt weak and dizzy and she wandered into the middle of the road and was nearly run down by a horse and carriage. The coachman cracked his whip angrily and shouted, 'Why can't you look where you're going, you stupid little girl!'

And the little match girl was so frightened and startled that she lost some of her precious matches in the snow.

As night approached, the blizzard increased in violence and even the fittest

She was nearly run down by a horse and carriage.

and strongest of the passers-by found it almost impossible to face the biting wind. They huddled inside their heavy over-coats and kept a tight grasp on their umbrellas to stop them from being tugged out of their hands by the cruel blizzard.

'I cannot stay here,' the little girl told herself desperately. 'I must leave the busy streets and find shelter.'

And she dragged her numbed feet away from the crowded pavements and stumbled on towards the quiet part of the big town where the rich people lived.

No one spared her a glance as she wandered away until presently she came to a road which was lined with tall, elegant houses.

How merry the ladies and their friends looked, as they laughed and raised their glasses to each other!

All the houses had lights streaming from their windows, and the little match girl heard the sound of laughter and the tinkling of glass against glass as the people inside toasted each other.

She looked around until she saw a small opening between two of the tall houses which would give her some shelter from the wind, and she went to it and sat down on the steps.

As she crouched there, she could see into one of the windows of the house opposite. How merry the ladies and their friends looked. How they laughed and shouted as they raised their glasses to each other!

And then there came to her the smell of roast goose. It was such a wonderful smell that the little girl closed her eyes in an effort to capture it. She almost forgot how hungry she was as she pictured the fat goose, roasted to a turn, sitting on the table.

There was no thought now in her mind of going home. It was so late that the lamps were all lit in the dark streets, and she had little hope of selling any of her matches. To go home at this hour, without any money, would bring down the anger of both her mother and her father on her head. And she dared not face that! If only her beloved grandmother had been alive —she would have protected her from her parents' anger. She would have drawn her within the shelter of her shawl and cuddled and kissed her and perhaps given her some tiny present which she had managed to make.

The little girl sighed deeply as she pulled the ragged shawl over her head. She would have to stay where she was for the rest of that night. In the morning it

She sat down in a small opening between two houses.

The match began to burn with a warm bright flame.

would be the first day of the New Year and perhaps then people would want to buy her matches.

But now her hands were so numb with cold that they had no feeling in them at all. She thought to herself that if only she could draw out one of her matches and rub it against the wall, its flame would warm her fingers.

It was not easy to do this, for her poor fingers were as stiff as boards, but at last she succeeded and she struck the match against the wall.

For an instant it sputtered and seemed to be going out. Then it began to burn with a warm bright flame.

'Why, it is like a Christmas candle!' the little girl thought. And it seemed to her that she was seated in a cosy armchair in front of a warm stove.

The room was small, but there were

*She cupped her hand round the
bright little flame and stared at the
magnificent stove.*

heavy curtains on the windows to shut out
the cold night air, and there was a pair of
woollen slippers, just her size, by the stove.

But the little girl did not think that
she had any need of the slippers so long as
the stove was there.

It was such a great big stove, all shiny
with polish, and it seemed to nod and
wink at her as it warmed her feet and her
hands and then her cold wet face.

'Oh, how lovely you are!' the little girl
whispered. 'How nice of you to warm me.
I have never felt so cosy.'

And she cupped her hand round the
bright little flame of her match as she
stared at the magnificent stove.

Alas, the match burned for just a
second longer and then it went out. The
big friendly stove vanished, and the little

girl found she had only the spent match
to look at.

'I must not, I dare not use any more of
the matches,' she told herself, as she put
the burned-out match on the step beside
her. 'But I will not throw this poor match
away for it brought me a lovely dream.'

Some hours passed and the little girl
began to wonder if she dared strike just
one more match.

She was so cold and weak that she
knew she would not be able to stand up to
do this, but then there was no need.

There was no one to see her wasting
her matches, for the gay party in the house
on the other side of the street was over. Or
perhaps the people had simply drawn the
curtains before sitting down to their roast
goose.

With fingers that were blue with cold
the little girl struck another match. It
burned up brightly and its light fell upon
the wall.

'Oh! How bright you are!' the little
girl exclaimed, her eyes fixed upon it.

And then the wall had vanished and

*She struck another match,
which burned up brightly.*

she found she could see into a room. And there on the table, which was laid with a snow-white cloth, was a wonderful fat roasted goose. It sat on a great silver dish and round it were roast potatoes.

There was stuffing, and two kinds of sauce, and there were dried sugar plums and all manner of delicious sweetmeats on the table besides the bird.

Then, wonder of wonders, the goose hopped off its silver dish and with a knife and fork in its beak waddled over to the little girl and invited her to take one of its wings.

'That's very kind of you,' the little girl began to say. 'Yes, please, I would like that, if you don't mind . . .' when, all

Wonder of wonders, the goose hopped off its silver dish.

at once the match spluttered and went out, and the goose vanished.

Tears came into the girl's eyes as she stared at the cold black wall. It had been such a wonderful sight—that snow-white table laden with so many good things to eat!

She knew now that it was not only the bitter weather which was making her feel so weak and helpless. It was also the fact that she had eaten nothing all day long. And without stopping to think she lit her third match.

Once again she found herself looking into a room. It was surely the finest room in the whole world and there in one corner stood the finest tree in the whole world. It was a thousand times more beautiful than any she had ever seen before.

Balls of different colours hung from its branches. And there were candles and shimmering tinsel which sparkled in the light, and from some of the lower branches there hung boxes tied up with pretty silk ribbon. It seemed as though the tree itself was alive.

As she stared at the wonderful tree, a little girl came into the room and she looked just like the match girl except that she was richly dressed in a cape and hood trimmed with fur.

As she stared at the wonderful tree, a little girl came into the room.

The match girl stretched out her hand to touch the beautiful young stranger, and suddenly the match went out, and the child and the Christmas tree were no longer to be seen.

As soon as her cold stiff fingers would permit, the girl lit another match against the wall and as the flame grew brighter she gave a cry of joy.

There, standing before her, was her own dear grandmother. She was so clear and so close that the little girl reached out to touch her, and the old woman held out her arms and smiled.

'Take me with you! Please take me!' the little girl pleaded. 'I've missed you so much and I want to be with you.'

Her grandmother's wise, gentle face was so kind and inviting that the little girl could not take her eyes away from it. And when her match was nearly ready to burn itself out, she began with frantic haste to strike another.

'Take me with you! Please take me!' the little girl pleaded.

*As her grandmother bore
her up to heaven . . .*

98

. . . her days of hunger and want were over for ever.

'Poor child!' he murmured.
'She has frozen to death!'

100

Each time her match had burned away she had lost something precious. Now at all costs she must keep her grandmother beside her.

But now the old woman was bending over her and gathering her up in her arms, and the little match girl sighed with a deep joy and thankfulness as she felt the warmth and comfort of her grandmother's arms about her. And as her grandmother bore her up to heaven the girl knew that all her days of hunger and want were over for ever.

Early the next morning, on the first day of the New Year, one of the gentlemen from the tall house opposite saw the little girl lying in the snow and he crossed the street to look at her.

'Poor child!' he murmured to himself. 'She has frozen to death. How sad for her!'

Then he saw all the burned matches in the snow and he thought to himself that she had lit them to warm her poor stiff fingers.

But there was something about the little girl which puzzled the old man. It was something about her face. It looked so smiling and peaceful.

'It was almost as if she had seen an angel,' said the old gentleman that night, as he sat cosily sipping wine with his wife by the fire. 'I tell you the child looked quite happy as she lay in the snow.'

'Don't bother your head about her any longer,' said his good wife sharply. 'It is the beginning of the year and there are a great many things to see to.'

And when her husband continued to stare dreamily into the flames and shake his old head, she clattered the fire-tongs noisily. 'There now!' she went on, annoyed that her husband was not paying her the attention she thought she deserved. 'Who cares about a match girl? The town is full of them and if I had my way I'd see to it that they were all kept at home in such terrible, wintry weather . . .'

'It may be,' said her husband mildly, 'that the child had nowhere to go. What on earth could have brought that smile to her face—it was such a happy one?'

And the old gentleman would continue to wonder—for how could he possibly guess that the little match girl had been smiling at someone as beautiful as her grandmother?

THE FROG PRINCE

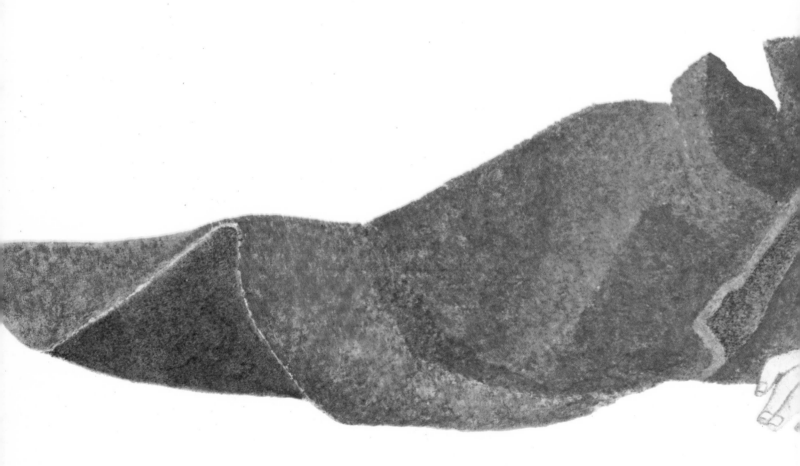

A long, long time ago, when the world was young and fresh, there lived a king whose family were all very beautiful.

Portraits of his beautiful wife and daughters were to be seen everywhere in his splendid castle, and the king delighted in pointing them out to visitors, but especially the pictures of his youngest child, for she was the most lovely of his daughters.

The young princess had hair that shone like spun gold in the sunshine and a skin which was as soft and smooth as the petals of a rose. She was so beautiful that some said she outshone the sun itself, which will give you some idea of how she was admired by all who saw her.

The king was so proud of his youngest child that he gave her many precious toys and among them was a wonderful golden ball which the princess treasured above her other costly playthings.

Every day, when the sun was doing its best to outshine her beauty, which it never did, she would take her golden ball into the royal forest. This forest bounded the king's castle on three sides. It was a very ancient forest and it contained an old well by which the princess liked to sit in the sunshine.

One morning the princess went as usual into the forest to sit by the well. But after a time she grew tired of sitting still and she began playing with her precious golden ball.

She tossed it in the air, smiling with pleasure as it glinted in the sun, and as it fell, she caught it in both hands. The game she was playing with her golden ball was one she had often played. But this morning she began tossing it higher and higher into the air.

And then, oh dear, she threw the ball upwards once too often, for when it came down, she failed to catch it. The ball dropped into the well with a huge splash and sank like a stone!

The young princess gave a gasp of dismay as she knelt down by the ancient well. She hoped that she might catch a glimpse of her precious ball. But it was just as if the well had swallowed it up. There was no sign of it.

'What shall I do? What shall I do?' the princess wailed aloud. And she was so unhappy at the thought of losing her most precious plaything that she began to cry. She was sobbing so bitterly that she did not notice the big ugly frog which had hopped out of the well and was sitting in the grass beside her.

The frog seemed to be waiting for her to speak to him and when she paid him no attention, he said, 'What's the matter with you? Why are you crying as if your heart would break?'

'My beautiful golden ball has fallen into this old well,' the princess replied, when she had managed to stifle her sobs. 'I loved it so much and now it's lost and I won't ever see it again.'

'I live down that old well,' said the frog. 'I daresay I could find your ball and bring it back to you . . .'

At this the princess gave a final sniff and dried her eyes. 'You—you really think you could?' she exclaimed. 'Oh do please try, dear frog. I would be so grateful!'

'You would have to make it worth my while,' said the frog. 'What would you give me if I did you this favour?'

'Well, you see I am a princess,' the girl began. 'Do you know what that means?'

'I knew you were a princess,' answered

The golden ball fell into the well.

the frog. 'You didn't have to tell me. I have often watched you playing here.'

'Then you will know that I can give you anything you ask for,' said the princess with a smile. 'What would you suggest? I can bring you my little golden crown if you like next time I come to the forest.'

'No thank you,' said the frog.

'I have a casket of pearls and rubies,' said the princess. 'You may have the casket if you wish.'

'No, I don't want your casket,' said the frog.

'Then what do you want?' demanded the princess impatiently.

'I want to be your playmate,' said the frog. 'I want to be invited to stay in the castle and sit with you at meals. If you let me eat from your plate and sleep in your

'I daresay I could find your ball and bring it back to you . . .'

little bed, then I will fetch the ball up from the bottom of the well.'

'But that is perfectly ridiculous!' the princess cried.

'If you say so,' replied the frog, and he made as if he meant to jump back into the well.

'Wait, wait!' the princess gasped. 'I will do as you say. You can be my very own playmate.' But even as she spoke she was thinking, 'Whoever heard of an ugly frog living in a castle? Once he fetches the ball I'll put him out of my mind.'

The frog did not guess what she was thinking and he hopped into the water and sank from sight.

The young princess clasped her hands, anxiously wondering if he would be clever enough to find her golden ball. And then she gave a shriek of joy when she spied the broad ugly face of the frog with the ball in his mouth. He swam to the edge of the well and hopped out, throwing the beautiful ball at her feet.

'Now carry me back to your castle,' said the frog.

But the princess shook her head as she picked up the ball. 'No, no, not today!' she murmured. 'But thank you very much for finding my plaything.'

And before the frog could remind her

She turned her back on him and set off through the forest.

of her promise, she turned her back on him and set off through the forest at a run, moving much too fast for the poor old frog.

'Wait, wait for me!' the frog cried in his ugly, hoarse voice. But the little princess did not even turn her head at the sound of his pleading croak.

'I do believe the silly creature meant what he said,' she thought, when at last she was safely home. 'I'll never play near that old well again for I don't ever want to set eyes on him.'

And she ran up to her own private room and put the golden ball in its special box by the window so that she could see

how pretty it was in the sunlight. Soon, as
she busied herself with brushing her soft
hair, she had quite forgotten the frog.

But the next day as she sat down to
dinner with her father the king, there
sounded a dull flippety-flop on the stairs
leading to the great door of the castle.

This dull flippety-flop noise was followed by a gentle knocking, and the king told the princess to go to the door and see who was outside.

As she ran to obey, she heard a voice crying, 'Youngest daughter of the king, let me in, let me in!'

The princess opened the door just a tiny crack, and when she saw the ugly old frog standing there on the step, she shut it again with all speed and ran back to the table.

'Who was it?' asked the king, as the princess sat down at her place and began eating from her little golden plate.

'Nothing — nobody,' she answered. 'It—it m-must have been the wind!'

But her father saw how the colour had fled from her cheeks and how, instead of eating properly, she toyed with her food, and so he asked again, 'Who was it, my child? Was it some terrible monster out there who frightened you?'

'No, no, not at all,' said the young princess. 'It was only a stupid ugly old frog. When I was playing by the well in the forest, I lost my golden ball. It fell into the water, and when I began crying at its loss, the frog offered to get it for me on condition that he became my little playmate. Why, he even made me promise to let him eat from my golden plate! It's really too ridiculous!' And the princess sniffed and tossed her head.

'It is not ridiculous,' said the king. 'You tell me you gave your promise to the frog. No daughter of mine must break her promise—even to a frog!'

Seeing the angry disappointed look on her father's face, the princess rose from the table and stood beside him. 'If I let the frog in,' she cried, 'he will try to sit at table with me and eat from my golden plate.' And she pouted crossly.

'If that is what you promised him, then that is what you must permit him to do,' said the king. 'Now go to the door and invite the frog inside.'

The princess hesitated, but she did not dare disobey her father and slowly she went over to the door and opened it.

The frog hopped inside and followed her back to the table. Then he said, 'I want to eat with you, youngest daughter of the king. Lift me on to your lap.'

'Do as he says,' her father ordered, and the princess lifted the clammy frog on to her lap and he began eating from her own golden plate.

The poor princess could not swallow a single morsel of her dinner and presently she placed the frog on a high chair so that he might eat at his leisure while she sat beside him and watched.

The frog ate with delicate care the delicious food that was set before him, and the beautiful princess could not take her eyes from him. 'What a dreadful creature he is,' she thought. 'I wish he could fall from the table and vanish. I wish I had never asked him to get my ball. I wish . . .' She was so busy with her spiteful thoughts that she scarcely heard the frog's polite request to be lifted down.

When she paid no attention to her unwelcome guest, the frog repeated his wish in a much louder more demanding croak. 'I have eaten until I can eat no more,' he said. 'Lift me down from the king's table, my little princess, and carry me upstairs to your silken bed.'

'I won't—I will not!' exclaimed the princess indignantly. 'You shan't sleep in my bed!'

But the king said gently, 'Do as the frog asks, daughter. Remember your promise!'

And, after a moment's hesitation, the princess picked up the clammy frog and carried him up to her room.

'I hate you, you nasty creature,' she exclaimed, staring down at the frog, and she was ready to burst into tears. 'What can I do with you? How can I rid myself of you?'

And she put the frog in a corner of her bedroom as far away from her silken bed as she could. But the frog said, 'Lay me in your silken bed, princess, or I will tell your father.'

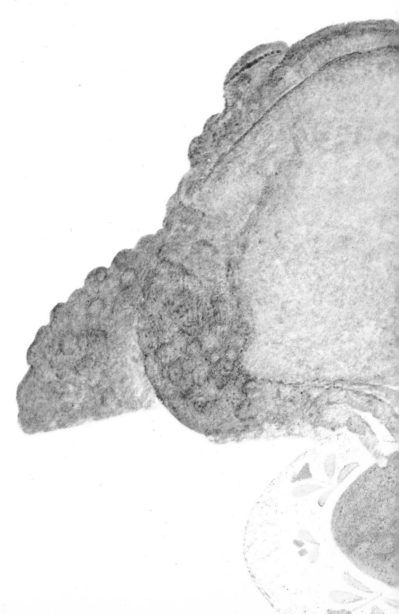

The princess could not take her eyes from him.

The frog changed into a tall noble young prince, richly clad in robes of silk.

The princess sobbed with anger and fear as once again she picked up the frog and carried him to her bed. Then, with a look of distaste, she put him between the silken sheets.

'Now climb in beside me,' said the frog. 'If you don't, I will tell the king.'

This was too much for the princess. With an angry scream she picked up the frog, and flung him with all her strength against the bedroom wall, at the same time crying, 'Hideous, horrible creature! I loathe and detest you . . .'

As she threw herself sobbing on the bed, something strange and wonderful took place. The frog, as he struck the wall, was no longer the clammy ugly creature he had been just seconds before, but a tall, noble young prince, richly clad in robes of silk.

The princess stared at the young man in amazement and, it must be confessed, in some shame. If she was to believe what her eyes were telling her, the handsome young man, with the kind friendly face, had once been a hideous frog. And she had treated the frog very shabbily!

'I—I am sorry . . .' she began. 'I—I did not guess . . .'

'You were not intended to,' said the prince with a smile. 'Some years ago a wicked fairy bewitched me and changed me into a frog. I was doomed to a life in the forest well until a lovely princess made me her guest . . .'

'But I didn't exactly do that,' put in the princess, blushing for shame.

'It was enough that you carried me to your room and with your own hands laid me in your bed,' said the prince. 'Now let us go together to your father, and ask him to allow us to marry.'

The princess was won over almost at once by the handsome prince who spoke with such kindness and she willingly agreed to ask her father's permission to marry him. This was given most willingly, for the king had only to look into the prince's eyes to see what a fine fellow he was.

The two young people then began making preparations for their wedding and on the day itself bells were rung from every church steeple announcing the happy event.

Never had the young princess looked more beautiful as she stood at the altar beside her handsome prince, and then indeed she did outshine the sun!

Early the next morning, when the pair were man and wife, there came to the castle a most magnificent coach to take the happy couple away to the prince's own

castle which stood in a neighbouring kingdom and which was even grander than
the king's.

The coach was drawn by eight splendid white horses with coloured plumes
fixed to their proud heads. At the back of
it rode one of the prince's most faithful
servants whose name was Henry.

When his master had been changed to
a frog by the wicked fairy, the devoted
Henry had three bands of iron placed
around his heart so that it would not break
from pity and grief.

*The coach was drawn by eight splendid white
horses with coloured plumes fixed to their proud
heads.*

Now, as the faithful servant assisted his royal master and the beautiful princess into the golden coach, there was the sound of splintering and cracking.

The princess looked round in alarm and the prince cried, 'Henry, Henry, is the coach safe to ride in?'

With a smile Henry replied,
'The bands from my heart have fallen in twain,
For long I suffered woe and pain.
While you a frog within a well
Enchanted by the witch's spell!'

And the Frog Prince gripped his loyal servant's hand before seating himself at the side of his new wife in the golden coach that was to carry them to their new home.

So ends the story of the beautiful young princess and the handsome Frog Prince. The princess grew more and more lovely with the passing of the years and, as was right and proper, the prince grew more and more loving. It is not surprising then that the royal couple lived for ever and ever in joy and happiness!

HANSEL AND GRETEL

Once upon a time, a very long time ago, there were two happy little children, a boy and a girl.

Their names were Hansel and Gretel, and they lived in a cottage on the edge of a big dark wood.

Hansel and Gretel often played in the woods because their father was a wood-cutter and sometimes, but not very often, he took his children with him when he set off for work.

Hansel knew the names of most of the pretty birds that sang in the trees, and Gretel had her own special friends among the busy squirrels and the shy rabbits.

'I wish—oh, how I wish that everything could stay the same for ever and ever,' Gretel would sometimes say.

And Hansel would answer, 'That's a silly kind of wish, little sister. Nothing stays exactly the same.'

Well, Hansel was right. One sad, sad day their mother became ill and, very shortly afterwards, she died.

For a time their father was too upset even to work. Then he met and married another woman, and put all his sadness behind him.

'Children,' said he, very gaily. 'Now you have a new mother who will love you and take care of you just as if she was your proper mother.'

The wood-cutter was wrong in thinking that he had chosen a kind, motherly woman as his new wife. She was not kind and she was not motherly and it became clear to the wood-cutter that he had made a mistake in asking her to be his wife.

Hansel and Gretel did their best to make their stepmother love them. But nothing they said or did pleased her.

To make matters worse the wood-cutter suddenly found that he was using up all his savings to keep his family in food. He could no longer count on selling his logs for a good price. The people in the surrounding villages could no longer afford to buy his firewood.

When the wood-cutter's wife saw how poor they were becoming, she began to grudge spending what money they had left on food for the children.

The wood-cutter loved his children and he was often very sad when he saw how hungry they were. But he was afraid of his wife and dared not say anything.

'Children,' said the wood-cutter, very gaily. 'Now you have a new mother who will love you and take care of you just as if she were your proper mother.'

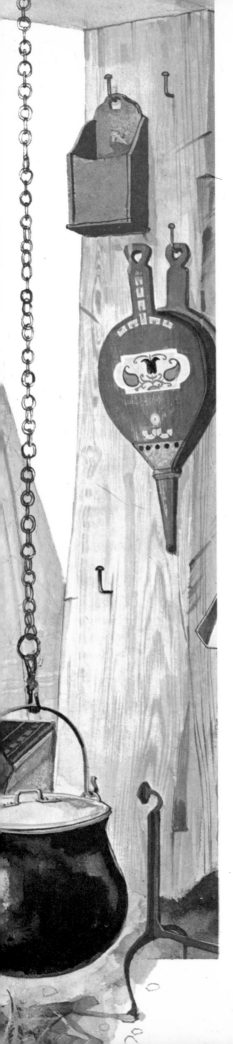

The wood-cutter buried his face in his hands when he heard his wife's cruel suggestion. And his wife, enraged, began to shout and scream at him.

Soon his wife began to give Hansel and Gretel black looks whenever they sat down to eat, and one dreadful night she said to her husband:

'We must rid ourselves of these two children of yours. They have such huge appetites that soon there will be nothing left for us to eat.'

The wood-cutter buried his face in his hands when he heard his wife's cruel suggestion. And his wife, enraged, began to shout and scream at him.

Her shouts roused the children and they crept downstairs to listen.

'Be as quiet as a mouse,' Hansel whispered to his sister. 'We mustn't let them know we are listening.'

They heard their father plead with his wife over and over again, but this only

Hansel filled his pockets with round shiny pebbles, as many as they would hold.

made her shout even more loudly.

At last she cried, 'We shall take them into the forest tomorrow and leave them there. They will never find their way home if we take them to a part where there are no familiar paths.'

When Hansel saw his poor father nod his head in agreement, he took his little sister's hand and together they crept back to bed.

'Don't worry,' he whispered, 'I have already thought of a plan.'

Long before his father and stepmother were awake, Hansel crept down the stairs

and out into the garden.

He filled his pockets with round, shiny pebbles, as many as they would hold, and then, very quietly, he went back into the house and up the stairs to bed.

Before the sun had properly risen he heard his stepmother call:

'Hansel, Gretel, get dressed at once and come downstairs! We are going to take you into the forest for a picnic.'

'Don't worry, little sister,' Hansel said, as Gretel began to cry. 'I have a plan and I know it will work.'

Their stepmother greeted them with a

sour smile when they appeared in the kitchen.

'Hurry,' she said. 'Eat this slice of bread now, and take another piece for your picnic.'

The children ate their bread quickly whilst their father got out his big axe.

Hansel's plan was working. So long as he could linger behind his stepmother he could go on dropping the pebbles.

Soon they were ready to set out, the wood-cutter leading the way into the dark, deep forest.

When they had walked for some little time, Hansel stopped and looked back.

'Hurry, you lazy boy,' said his step-mother over her shoulder.

*The children ate their bread
and shared some of it with
the two friendly squirrels.*

'I just wanted to see if our cat was on
the cottage roof,' said Hansel.

As he spoke he dropped one of his
shiny white pebbles on the grass. His plan
was working. So long as he could linger
behind his stepmother he could go on
dropping his pebbles.

Hansel had no idea how far they
walked that day. When his father stopped
at last they were in a strange part of the
forest and miles and miles from home.

'We have gone far enough,' said the
wood-cutter with a sad, bitter smile.

'Rest here, children, whilst your
mother and I go farther into the forest to
gather wood.'

'They will not come back for us,'
Gretel whispered fearfully.

'Don't worry, little sister,' Hansel
said, taking her hand. 'I have laid a trail of

When it was beginning to grow dark Hansel took his sister's hand and led her through the trees.

shiny white pebbles. The pebbles will show us the way home.'

Then the children ate their bread and shared some of it with two friendly squirrels.

'We must wait for a time,' Hansel said, when they had eaten. 'We must not arrive at our cottage before they do!' And he laughed so cheerfully that Gretel laughed too.

'How clever you are, Hansel,' she smiled. 'Now I'm sure we shall get home safely and I'm no longer afraid.'

When it was beginning to grow dark Hansel took his sister's hand and led her through the trees.

'Look! Can you see?' he cried. 'How brightly the pebbles shine even in the dark! Soon the moon will be riding high in the sky and then my pebbles will look

*They crept to the top of the stairs and
listened and listened . . .*

like gleaming silver pennies.'

When the moon came out at last it was
easier than ever to find the pebbles and in
no time at all, it seemed to Hansel, their
cottage was in sight and they were home.
How wonderful to be home!

What a warm, welcoming hug their
father gave them, and how darkly did their
stepmother scowl as she stared at them.
But Hansel and Gretel cared nothing for
her black looks. They were safely home
and that was all that mattered!

All was peaceful in the little house for
some weeks and then one night, just as the
children were going to sleep, they heard
the harsh voice of their stepmother
raging again at their father.

'We must find out if she is trying to
persuade him to lose us again in the

How quickly their stepmother walked as she pushed the children in front.

forest,' Hansel whispered to Gretel. 'Come on, let's listen to what they are saying . . .'

So they crept to the top of the stairs and they listened and they listened. And, sad to say, they heard their father murmur, 'Oh, very well, wife. We shall take them into the forest early in the morning. And this time, I promise you, they shall not find their way home.'

Hansel waited until his parents had gone to bed. Then he crept downstairs expecting to find the back door unlocked. But this time the door was locked and barred and, no matter how hard he tried, he could not turn the big heavy key.

'You must save your bread,' he told

'As soon as the moon appears in the sky we shall set out for home,' said Hansel. 'Let's try to sleep.'

Presently the moon came out but, search as he might, Hansel could not find a single breadcrumb.

Gretel in the morning, as they were setting out. 'I will lay a trail of breadcrumbs. The crumbs will show up just as well as the pebbles did.'

Gretel nodded her little head and promised that she would not eat her share of the bread but give it to Hansel before they set out.

How quickly their stepmother walked as she and the wood-cutter pushed the children in front of them through the woods.

But soon Hansel and Gretel were able to run ahead, and then Hansel was able to drop his breadcrumbs in secret places.

This time the wood-cutter took his children a great long way into the forest to a quiet, dark, deserted place.

'Rest here,' he told them at last. 'Your mother and I'll go a little farther on, and then we shall come back for you.' And he kissed them tenderly.

'He won't come back. I know he won't!' Gretel cried.

'It doesn't matter,' Hansel said cheerfully. 'I've laid a splendid trail of breadcrumbs. As soon as the moon appears in the sky, we shall set out for home. Let's try to sleep.'

When the children awoke, it was dark. Presently the moon came out but, oh dear, search as he might, Hansel could not find a single breadcrumb. The little birds had found the bread first and eaten up every bit of it.

How dark and scary it was in that thick gloomy wood, and how wildly did the children run, this way and that—and

The little birds had found the bread first and eaten up every bit of it.

all the time, had they but known it, they were going farther and farther away from their own little cottage!

At last they were so tired that even Hansel was ready to give up. They had walked most of the night and now it was morning again, and they were so weary and so hungry they thought they would surely die. And then, just when Gretel was ready to burst into tears, she saw a beautiful snow-white bird sitting in a tree.

'Goodness!' shouted Hansel. 'It's a house made of bread and covered with cake and icing and sugary biscuits!'

'Look, Hansel,' she whispered, 'that pretty white bird seems to be trying to tell us something. How sweetly it sings. I think it wants us to follow it.'

As she spoke, the white bird spread its wings and flew just a little way, and Hansel and Gretel followed it. It led them to the most wonderful little house they had ever seen.

'Goodness!' shouted Hansel, 'It's a house made of bread and covered with

Soon the children were seated at the table and eating all the nicest things imaginable.

cake and icing and sugary biscuits!'

Gretel clapped her hands and shrieked with delight, all her tiredness forgotten.

'Clever bird!' she cried. 'It has led us to this wonderful cake house. Ooh, I'm so hungry! Look, Hansel, the porch has pillars of gorgeous sticky rock. Isn't it tempting! Let's try the sugary cake walls first . . .'

As they began to help themselves to the cake house the door opened suddenly, and out came a motherly old woman. She had a soft, purring voice and bright red eyes and she walked with a stick.

'Come in, dear children,' she said softly. 'You like nibbling at my house, but wait until you see what I have for you inside. You can feast on sugared buns and apples and pears and delicious cakes all

day long if you wish.'

'We're lost, and we'd love to come inside,' said Hansel, his mouth full of cake. 'Thank you very much.'

So the children went into the cake house and soon they were seated at the table and eating all the nicest things imaginable. The old lady watched them with a kindly expression on her gnarled and wrinkled face.

'Eat up, my dears,' she would say, whenever Hansel or Gretel vowed they couldn't eat or drink anything more. 'I like my children to be round and plump.' And she would give the oddest little chuckle, as if she were sharing a secret joke with herself.

'How lucky we are to have you,' said Hansel at last. 'May we stay here just for

The old woman watched over them until they had fallen sound asleep.

one night? Then tomorrow you will perhaps guide us to the path that will lead us out of this deep forest.'

The old woman made no answer, but presently she showed Hansel and Gretel where they would sleep.

And when they were safely tucked up in their beds, she watched over them until they had fallen sound asleep.

Then, and only then, did she allow herself to cackle loudly and, as she hobbled about the room, chuckling and talking to herself, her red eyes blazed with greed and spite.

The old woman, you see, was none other than the most wicked witch you can imagine, and her wonderful cake house was simply there to trap little children. Whenever she was hungry she sent out her pet white bird to look for little boys and girls, just like Hansel and Gretel. How fortunate it was that her bird had per-

formed so well, for it was a long time now since she had managed to catch two such pleasant children. No wonder she smiled and chuckled as she prepared the cage into which she would put young Hansel in the morning.

Poor Hansel! He could scarcely believe what was happening to him when the wicked witch carried him away early the next morning and thrust him into the small wooden cage. This horrid cage was anchored to the floor of the witch's tower with strong chains.

'Let me out! Let me out!' Hansel screamed, when he saw his sister.

'I can't help you, brother,' she replied. 'We are in the power of a witch who eats little children. Now she has forced me to be her servant.'

'Let me out! Let me out!' Hansel screamed when he saw his sister.

134

'Hansel, let me feel if your finger grows faster,' asked the witch every day.

Hansel shook the bars of his prison, but they were so thick and set so closely together that he soon gave up. He would never move them.

'We must think of another way to save ourselves,' he told Gretel. 'Do whatever the old witch asks of you, and don't despair.'

It was hard to do everything the witch asked because now she expected Gretel to do all the fetching and carrying, all the washing and sweeping of floors.

'I'm far too busy cooking for that brother of yours,' the witch would cackle. 'He must have the best of everything and all of it must be cooked with butter and cream. Oh-ho, it won't be long before he is fat enough to roast and eat.'

Gretel had nothing but crab-shells and stale crusts to eat, for the witch had decided she would never make a tasty meal to enjoy.

Every day for a week the witch paid a visit to Hansel.

Now, you may not know, but witches with very red eyes do not see very clearly. The wicked witch of the cake house had red, red eyes and she did not see at all well, which was very lucky for Hansel.

Each time the old woman went to the cage and said, 'Hansel, let me feel if your finger grows fatter,' Hansel thrust out a little chicken bone for her to feel.

After three weeks, the wicked witch could not hide her disappointment from little Gretel.

'That brother of yours eats like a lord,' she said angrily, 'and yet he grows no fatter. Ah well, I shall eat him tomorrow. I cannot wait any longer for my feast.'

Then she sent Gretel into the yard to fetch water and, when she returned, told her to get out the largest dishes and biggest bowls, because she had a mind to make a tasty sauce and wished to have all the various ingredients ready mixed for tomorrow's dinner.

How Gretel wept as she was forced to obey the wicked witch. How she pleaded and begged for mercy for her brother! But the witch only laughed and seemed very pleased at the sight of her tears.

Early the next morning the witch set about preparing for her feast.

'I have a mind to bake first,' she said to Gretel. 'Light the fire and I will heat up the oven.'

The witch began to bake and, as she kneaded the dough, she called out to Gretel to go to the oven, open the door and see if it was heating up nicely.

'The door is too big and heavy for me to open,' said Gretel. 'And I'm too small to look inside.'

'Stupid child!' muttered the old witch. 'I will look for myself!' And she went over to the big oven in the wall and thrust her head inside.

Silent as a mouse, Gretel crept up behind and, with all her strength, pushed the old witch deep inside her own oven. Then she shut and bolted the great iron door in the wall.

So that was the end of the wicked red-eyed witch. Gretel quickly found the key to Hansel's prison and set him free.

Gretel pushed the old witch inside her oven, then shut and bolted the great iron door in the wall.

Soon Hansel was filling his pockets with gold and precious stones taken from the witch's treasure chests.

'The witch is dead,' she told him excitedly. 'And I know where she keeps all her treasure.'

Soon Hansel was filling his pockets with gold and precious stones taken from the witch's treasure chests, while Gretel waited by the door.

Then they left that dreadful house and set out for home. They had walked for two hours or more when they came, at last, to a great wide lake. And at the sight of so much water, Gretel cried out in despair, 'Oh, Hansel, what shall we do? We can't swim and there isn't a bridge or a boat anywhere in sight.'

As she spoke, a lovely white swan came

Hansel waded out into the water and climbed on the swan's back.

swimming straight towards them.

'Please take us across this wide, wide lake,' Gretel said to the graceful white bird. And Hansel waded out into the water and climbed on its back. The swan opened its wings so that Hansel could sit safely, then took him across the lake before returning to ferry Gretel across.

So, thanks to the bird, Hansel and Gretel were carried across the water and, to their surprise and delight, very soon spied their own little cottage through a gap in the trees.

'Look, there's father!' Gretel shouted in delight as the wood-cutter appeared on the doorstep of the old cottage.

With cries of joy both children ran into his outstretched arms.

Oh, what happiness, to be hugged and kissed and drawn into the cosy kitchen where Hansel told his amazing story!

When the wood-cutter had heard it at least three times over and seen all the witch's treasure, he said:

'Your stepmother left me. She did not love me after all.'

'We love you, father,' said Gretel, her eyes shining like stars.

'And you love us,' said Hansel. 'You didn't want to leave us all alone in the dark forest, did you?'

'Indeed not,' said the wood-cutter.

'Then let us all be happy together,' said Hansel, holding up a gleaming necklace of diamonds. 'The witch's treasure will take care of all our wants for ever and ever, and we will be able to help all our poor friends in the village whenever they need it.

And so it proved!

With cries of joy the children ran into their father's outstretched arms.

PUSS-IN-BOOTS

There was once a miller who had three sons. The miller worked so hard all his life that you might have expected him to die a rich man. But this was not so, and there was so little in his last Will and Testament that his sons did not even bother to consult a lawyer. The mill itself went to the eldest. The donkey went to the second son. And the miller's cat, a sly puss if ever there was one, went to the miller's youngest.

'Father could do no less than leave me the mill,' said the eldest son, as they stood outside the mill discussing their inheritance. 'After all I was his right-hand man. And he knew I would be able to keep it going.'

'Of course you will,' said the second son, with a great deal of enthusiasm, for he hoped and prayed his brother would ask him to stay on. Then he added, 'I admit I expected more than the donkey, but he's a useful, willing beast and our father thought highly of him.'

'I know what is in your mind,' said his brother. 'And the answer is yes, you can stay here with me. There will be plenty of work for both you and the donkey.'

The two brothers shook hands and both were happy that they had come to such a satisfactory arrangement.

Watching them, the miller's youngest son was filled with envy. Clearly he was not going to be asked to say on at the mill. He must now try and make his own way in the world. But what could he do? All he had was the cat. And he had never heard of a cat making any man's fortune!

'You're no more use to me than a sack of flour,' he said crossly, as his cat came up to him and rubbed himself against his leg. 'Oh, I know you are a cunning and skilful hunter of mice and that it doesn't take much to keep you. But you're just no use to me now that I have to leave the mill and find some work.'

Now if the miller's son had really and truly studied his cat, he would have seen what bright blue eyes he had, and he might even have wondered why the cat seemed to want his company so much.

Wherever he went, along came the cat as if determined not to be left out of anything, no matter what . . .

At last when the youth had nearly trodden on the cat's tail not once but several times, he exclaimed in a bad-tempered voice, 'Will you go away and leave me! Stop following me around!'

'Don't send me away,' said the cat, and strange to say the miller's son felt no surprise at hearing his cat speak. 'It is true I am only a cat, but if you will only trust me I'll make your fortune.'

'*Too bad you have to go,' said he with a grin on his face.*

'Make my fortune!' As if this idea was too silly to consider, the youth shook his head and sat down, and the cat sprang into his lap and settled himself comfortably just as the miller's second son came along with his donkey.

'Too bad you have to go,' said he with a grin on his fat round face. 'But there is nothing else you can do. Anyway,' he added cheerfully, 'you have the cat for company. He's a good mouser, that one...'

'Yes, yes, I have the cat,' his young brother answered bitterly. 'And what do you suggest I do with him?'

'Why not sell him,' came the reply. 'If I were you I'd sell him for his skin. He'll fetch a good price in the town. Why not think about it, old boy? There's nothing much else you have to sell, is there? And there is quite a market for skins if they are in good condition.'

The miller's son looked thoughtful as he considered this new idea. But as soon as his brother had gone, his cat said, in a soft, purring voice, 'I wouldn't do that, if I were you. I shall be of no use to you at all if you sell me for my skin. Now, if only

The cat sprang on to his lap and settled himself comfortably.

'First, I would like a pair of high leather boots. Then you may call me Puss-in-Boots.'

you will promise to take care of me and do as I ask, why then, I will take care of *you* and make your fortune for you . . .'

The cat spoke so earnestly and so solemnly that the miller's son began to believe in him.

'What do you ask of me?' he demanded, after staring at him for a moment.

'It is not so very much,' said the cat. 'First, I would like a pair of high leather boots. Then you may call me Puss-in-Boots. Second, I would like a sack.'

'I suppose I could spend the last of my money on a pair of boots for you,' said the young man. 'And as for the sack—well, I can get that from the mill.'

'Then it's a bargain,' purred the cat, looking very smug.

That same day the miller's son went to market and spent most of his savings on a very fine pair of boots. Puss was so pleased with them that he put them on right away, saying, 'They will do very nicely. They are just what I wanted.'

'I hope so,' said his master in a voice full of doubt, for already he was wondering if he had been wise to trust his cat. Then he added more brightly. 'And here is your sack. At least that didn't cost me any money. What do you want with it?'

'Help me fill it with tasty, sweet bran,'

ordered Puss-in-Boots. 'Then I shall be on my way, for if I'm going to make your fortune, Master, the sooner I set about it the better!'

'I agree!' cried the miller's son. 'I won't ask you what you mean to do with a sack full of bran, or even where you mean to go with it.'

'There is no mystery about where I am going,' replied Puss-in-Boots in a very confident way. 'I'm off to the woods where I hope to do some hunting.'

Now for the life of him the cat's master could not think how this would in any way improve his fortune. So he did not wish his cat good luck. But went off to seek an old hut where he thought he might shelter for a day or two.

Meanwhile Puss, with his sack slung

'I'm off to the woods where I hope to do some hunting.'

He lay beside the sack and pretended to be very fast asleep.

over his back, went off into the woods and to test his fine new boots he plunged into all the brambles and nettles he could find on the way.

When he reached a spot where he knew there were a great many warrens which held a great many plump young rabbits, he arranged his sack on the ground, with its neck wide open and the string, which would close the neck, firmly held in his paw. Then he lay down beside the sack, from which came an inviting smell of bran, and pretended to be very fast asleep.

Presently a young foolish little rabbit, who was not nearly old enough to have learnt how to take care of himself, came hopping along. He sniffed the bran and being very greedy hopped inside the sack after it. Puss lay perfectly still until the rabbit was well and truly inside. Then with a sudden lifting of his paw and a sharp tug, he closed the neck of the sack and made the little rabbit his prisoner.

Well, that was the end of that poor foolish greedy little rabbit. And the very beginning of Puss-in-Boots' visits to the palace. He knew, you see, that the king was very fond of rabbit pie.

'I have brought you a fine plump rabbit, Your Majesty,' he said, when he gained admittance to the king. 'It will make an excellent pie or stew.'

'How thoughtful!' cried the king, who was extremely fond of his food. 'And who sent you with such a splendid gift, may I ask? Pray tell me.'

'My master, the Marquis of Carabas,' said Puss-in-Boots, thinking what a really splendid name that was to invent.

'Then thank him most kindly,' said the king, with a gracious smile.

Now for a whole month or more Puss came regularly to the palace and always he had some gift for the king. Sometimes it

'I have brought you a fine plump rabbit, Your Majesty.'

149

was a rabbit, sometimes it was a pheasant or a partridge. And, of course, whenever the delighted king asked for the name of the sender of such welcome gifts, the cat replied, 'The Marquis of Carabas!'

Puss soon learnt from the palace servants that the king had a beautiful daughter and that once a week he took the princess out riding in his coach.

'I want you to do exactly as I tell you,' he said one day to his master.

'What do you want me to do?' asked the young man curiously.

'You must go and bathe in the river at a spot I will show you.'

'Oh, very well!' agreed his master, and he followed his cat to the river. No sooner was he in the water than Puss promptly hid his shabby old suit under a big stone, and settled down to wait for the king's coach. When it came, Puss began shouting at the top of his voice, 'Help! Help! My noble master, the Marquis of Carabas is drowning! Save him! Save him!'

'Help! Help! The Marquis of Carabas is drowning!'

The escorts hauled the noble young lord out of the river.

Now, thanks to Puss-in-Boots, the king was no stranger to the name of the Marquis of Carabas. When he heard the cat's anxious shouts for help and saw the young man in the river, he ordered his coach to stop at once, and his two escorts to haul the noble young lord out of the river.

'Bless my soul!' exclaimed the king, as the miller's son was rescued. 'What great good fortune it was that I came this way!'

'If you please, Your Majesty,' Puss whispered in his ear. 'My noble master has had his clothes stolen. Would it be in your power to send for a suit to the palace? Otherwise he cannot . . .'

'Certainly, certainly,' replied the king. And he despatched his escorts to his palace with instructions to bring back a fine suit of clothes for the young man.

When the miller's son was dressed in his borrowed clothes, he certainly looked every inch a lord, and the king graciously invited him to ride in his coach.

As soon as Puss-in-Boots saw his master seated beside the beautiful young princess, he sped off down the road.

So far his plan had worked entirely to his satisfaction. But there was still much to be done!

Puss-in-Boots was running so fast that he almost passed the two labourers who were working by the side of the road. The two countrymen gaped at the cat in his high boots, and their astonishment grew when Puss stopped and stared at them fiercely. Then with a snarl he said, 'You know all that land behind you? All these forests and fields?'

'Yes, sir,' said one. 'They belong to our lord and master.'

'Oh no they don't,' Puss snapped. 'They belong to the Marquis of Carabas! And when the king comes this way, you

must tell him so. If you don't, I'll return and chop you up into mincemeat, then eat you!'

Well this was too much for the two men. They saw what sharp teeth the cat had, and how long and terrible were his claws, and they gave their solemn promise that they would do what he asked.

Well pleased, Puss-in-Boots ran on just as the king's coach came in sight. Now the king was not only a jolly fellow but he was also quite a greedy one. And he was most anxious that his daughter, the lovely princess, should marry a very rich young lord. In that way he would gain even more land than he had at present.

From time to time he looked at the young man in the coach very thoughtfully. He was certainly handsome, and it seemed to him that his daughter was attracted to him. They made a fine couple as they sat side by side. He didn't think it would be long before they fell in love. But first he must find out if the marquis was as rich as

'Tell the king the lands belong to the Marquis of Carabas!'

he thought he might be, though he could not, of course, ask him.

'Stop the coach,' he commanded suddenly, as they were passing the labourers. 'I want to speak to these two workers.'

The coach came to a stop and the king put his head out of the window and asked, 'Who owns all this land behind you?'

'The Marquis of Carabas,' replied the two men in one voice. Then one of them added. 'Yes, Your Majesty, all the land is owned by the noble Marquis!'

'*The Marquis of Carabas,*'
replied the men in one voice.

At this the king smiled very kindly on the young man at his daughter's side, and he did not even frown when presently he saw that they were holding hands.

Meantime Puss-in-Boots had been speaking to a group of haymakers in a rich meadow. And they too were quite terrified by his terrible threat to chop them up into mincemeat.

'Now don't forget,' he warned them, 'I will return if you do not obey me.'

Well, the king smiled even more graciously when the workers in the golden meadow cried, 'This meadow and all the meadows around belong to the Marquis of Carabas, Your Majesty!' in answer to his question.

'That is good news indeed,' said the king as he ordered the coach to drive on, and he began to wonder what kind of

'What about something really big?' said Puss.

castle the marquis lived in. It would certainly be worth finding out.

As luck would have it the only castle the royal coach was likely to pass belonged to an ogre who was also a very powerful magician. Puss knew all about this and he worked out a plan to make an end of him.

'I have heard,' said he, when he was in the ogre's presence, 'that you have most remarkable powers. They say you can turn yourself into any animal you choose.'

'That's true,' said the ogre.

'What about something really big?' said Puss. 'Perhaps a beast that lives in the jungle?'

Scarcely had he spoken than Puss

found himself facing a huge lion, which so terrified him that he jumped out of the castle window on to the sloping roof.

Shaking with fright he could not bring himself to climb back into the room and face those cruel, gaping jaws until he heard the ogre laughing.

'You may come back,' shouted the ogre, between gusts of laughter. 'I won't eat you. But now you know my powers!'

'I do indeed,' said the cat, as he jumped down from the window. 'You are the

He was terrified of the huge lion.

most wonderful magician I have ever met in my whole life.' He paused, then went on somewhat timidly. 'I suppose for a man of your great size a lion was quite easy. It would be far harder to turn yourself into something really tiny . . .'

'Makes no difference,' said the ogre with confidence. 'What would you suggest?'

'I—I thought perhaps a little mouse,' said Puss-in-Boots.

The ogre laughed again. 'Well, I don't see why not!' he chuckled. And straight away there was a little grey mouse in the middle of the room!

Puss-in-Boots smiled wickedly. Then he pounced, and that was the end of the mouse, and the end of the poor old ogre who had tried to show off once too often!

'Welcome to the castle of the Marquis of Carabas!'

Now Puss had the castle to himself and he ran into the banqueting hall to satisfy himself that the table was laid and there was food to offer the royal party.

He was waiting at the castle gates when the king's coach appeared and, with an air of importance, he cried, 'Welcome, Your Gracious Majesty, welcome to the castle of the Marquis of Carabas!'

'Magnificent! Quite magnificent!' the king exclaimed, as he stepped down from the coach and saw how grand the castle was. 'But it is no more than I expected.'

In high good humour he asked Puss if they could expect any refreshments.

'Indeed yes, Your Majesty,' said Puss, knowing that the late ogre had a very well-stocked larder. 'Although my master was not expecting you, there is plenty to eat and drink.'

'That's good news,' laughed the king, for he was feeling peckish after his long ride. 'Lead the way, my dear Puss-in-Boots. Your master may take my daughter's arm!'

Well, it must be admitted that the visit to the castle was an enormous success, and if the miller's son remained unusually silent it might have been because he was so very much in love with the princess.

In fact the king took this to be the reason, and he gave his daughter a little nudge, in secret, just to let her know that she had his blessing if, by chance, she too was falling in love!

'Why don't we all return to my palace?' his majesty said at last. 'I'd like the Marquis to meet my lady wife, the queen. She may want to ask him a few questions.'

When Puss heard this, he knew that the fortunes of his master were made. And of course he was perfectly right.

That same evening, as they all sat down to dinner, the queen enquired if

Puss-in-Boots was now the most contented cat alive.

their handsome young guest was free to marry. And to this the miller's son could truthfully answer, yes.

Well, in no time at all the princess and the miller's youngest son were happily married. And Puss was given a new pair of high boots to match the colour of his eyes for the wedding.

His home was now the palace and, as the months went by, he became a great favourite at court, the ladies spoiling him with specially prepared dishes of chicken and saucers of thick cream.

No wonder Puss-in-Boots was the most contented cat alive! No wonder he purred all day! He had made his master's fortune and he had made his own at the same time. What more could he ask!

THE GOOSEGIRL

There was once a queen who had a beautiful daughter who was dearer than all the world to her. The girl had hair of gold and eyes that were as blue as a summer sea.

Everybody liked the princess because she was always happy and cheerful, and always kind to those she met. However, there was someone who did not like the princess, and that was her maid. The maid was terribly jealous of her mistress. She was jealous of the beautiful clothes the princess wore and of the royal horse from the royal stables that she went out riding on. But what she most envied the princess for was that she never had to do anything. Everything was done for the princess—absolutely everything.

When the princess rose in the morning, it was her maid who filled her bath and perfumed the water. It was the maid who laid out the princess's clothes ready for her and sewed on any buttons that had come off. Every morning she combed the princess's tresses of gold, and when her hair shone like the rays of the sun it was the maid who set the coronet on her mistress's head.

'If only I were a princess,' the maid thought, 'then I wouldn't have to go on doing all this work.'

One day the queen decided that it was time to look for a husband for the princess. This was not at all easy, for the queen thought that even the best of young men could not be good enough for her lovely daughter. She sent for princes from all countries, near and far, to come to the court. But one prince would be too old, another too fat, and a third not really handsome enough. But at last she heard of a prince in a far-off land who she thought was a suitable young man for her daughter to marry, and she began to make the arrangements with the prince's father.

The day of the wedding was fixed and then the queen sent for her daughter to tell her the news. The queen could not help feeling rather sad. She would miss her dear daughter greatly when she had gone. Since the old king had died the two of them had become especially dear to each other.

'I have chosen a good husband for you,' the queen told the princess 'He is the son of a mighty king and he lives a

'I have chosen a good husband for you,'
the queen told the princess 'He is the son
of a mighty king and he lives a long way
from here.'

long way from here.'

The princess nodded. She had already guessed what was to happen, because in the last few days dozens of trunks had been packed with her trousseau and all her gold and jewels. She had also had to try on a lot of new dresses, which she found very boring. But now everything was ready. She was going to make a long journey and soon after that she was going to be a bride. That night the princess was so excited she could hardly sleep.

The next day the princess said goodbye to her mother.

'I have had my best horse saddled for you,' said the queen. 'He is called Falada and he will take you to the far country where the prince lives. He is a very special horse. I have also ordered your maid to travel with you for company and there is a horse ready for her too. Finally, I want to give you this handkerchief. You must always keep it on you, for it can help you if you are ever in trouble.'

The evening before, the queen had cut her finger so as to let three drops of her blood fall on to the silk handkerchief. Now, as she gave it to her daughter, she warned her once again, 'Remember, don't lose it!' Then they parted.

The princess set out on the long journey in cheerful spirits. The weather was fine and she was delighted by everything she saw, the flowers, the birds, the butterflies, the rabbits . . . for the princess

was very fond of all living creatures.

The maid rode ahead of the princess and every now and then she turned and looked back with a discontented expression on her face.

'If I could wear those beautiful clothes that the princess has, then I would look much prettier than she does,' the girl thought to herself. 'And then there's her horse! I hate to see her riding on such a fine animal while I have to make do with this old nag. But I shall think of something. Just give me the chance and then we shall see . . .'

The princess had no idea that her maid was hatching evil plans. She was hot now from riding and she wanted something to drink. So in a friendly tone

The princess was delighted by all she saw.

of voice she asked the maid, 'Would you please fill my gold cup with water from that stream over there? I'm so thirsty!'

'Fill it yourself,' the maid answered rudely and spitefully. 'I'm not working my fingers to the bone for you any more.'

'Whatever next?' the astonished princess thought to herself. But then she shrugged her shoulders. 'I expect she did not sleep very well last night. I'll get the water myself.'

When she went to mount her horse Falada again, the animal said:

'Your good heart is tender and dear,
But wicked and wily your maid.
But to me the future is clear—
They'll all come to nothing,
The terrible plans she has laid.'

'Have no fear, Falada,' said the princess. 'So long as I have the handkerchief my mother gave me, the maid can do me no harm.'

The princess mounted the horse and rode on, quite carefree again. She soon forgot what had happened with the maid.

About the middle of the day the princess was thirsty again. Without thinking she once again asked the maid, 'Would you please fetch me a cup of water?'

'I've told you once already that I'm not going to go on working my fingers to the bone for the likes of you.'

Without saying a word, the princess got down from her horse and ran to the stream. She bent over the water—and she dropped the handkerchief her mother

'Have no fear, Falada,' said the princess. 'So long as I have the handkerchief my mother gave me, the wicked maid can do me no harm.'

had given her, and it quickly floated away down the stream! The princess had not noticed her loss, but the maid had.

'Just you wait a minute,' she said when the princess was about to mount her horse again. 'Take those clothes off. I want to wear them.'

Only then did the princess discover that she had lost the handkerchief, and now she was powerless.

'That's better!' said the maid when she had put on the princess's fine clothes. 'Now I'm going to take Falada and you can ride my horse.' But when he heard this, Falada began to buck and rear, kicking out with his hooves, so that the maid had to keep riding her old horse after all.

'Now I'm going to take
Falada and you can ride my
horse,' said the maid when
she had put on the princess's
fine clothes.

When they had reached the country where the prince lived, and had arrived at the royal court, the wicked maid acted as if she was the princess. The prince kissed her hand courteously, but he was very

When they arrived at the royal court, the wicked maid acted as if she was the princess.

disappointed. He had hoped that his bride would be prettier than this girl in front of him. Could this be the lovely princess of whom his father had told him? The prince thought she looked very dis-

The prince kissed the maid's hand.

contented and disagreeable.

'And tell me, who is that?' he asked, pointing to the real princess.

'Oh, that's my maid,' said the maid. 'I brought her with me to keep me company, but she annoys me now. I don't want her near me any more. Let her go and work in the kitchens or the stables.'

The prince looked at the fine delicate hands of the real princess and said, 'She certainly won't do for that kind of work. She would do better looking after the geese.'

So the princess had to take the geese to the meadow, with a rude boy called Kurt for company.

So the princess had to take the geese to the meadow.

When the princess came home from the meadow, she saw the head of her horse over the gateway.

'I don't understand why you have to come with me,' said the boy. 'I can tend the geese quite all right by myself, and you don't look as if you have ever been a goosegirl before.'

The princess did not answer. She was thinking of how her maid would be sitting next to the prince at the banquet.

The next day, when she was walking with the geese past the royal stables, she heard her maid saying to the prince, 'That horse should be put down,' and the maid was pointing to Falada.

'Why?' asked the prince in astonishment.

'Because he is a bad horse, wild and headstrong, and no one can really manage him,' answered the maid.

'Very well, then, he will be sent for slaughter,' the prince said.

Naturally the real princess was filled with sorrow when she heard that Falada was to be killed. 'If only I could go to the prince and tell him that I am the real princess,' she thought. But she dared not do this, for she was afraid he would not believe her; and in any case the maid had already threatened that she would have her put to death if she said anything. No, she could do nothing to save her horse. However, she would go to the slaughter-house and ask for Falada's head to be put over the palace gates.

That evening, when the princess came home from the meadow, she saw the head of her horse over the gateway. She said, 'Oh, why have they done this to us and what will happen next?'

And the horse's head answered:
> 'Tender and dear is your good heart,
> princess,
> Wicked and wily, princess, is your
> maid.
> Let's hope that the plans she has
> cunningly laid,
> Will soon be made plain and have
> no more success.'

Kurt, who was walking behind the princess, listened in astonishment to all this. What a strange girl this was! She talked to a horse's head—and the horse's head answered! It gave him the shivers.

The next morning exactly the same thing happened. The girl spoke to the

horse's head and again the horse's head answered.

A little later, when they were in the meadow with the geese, the princess took off her hat to comb her hair.

How Kurt stared and stared! 'That hair looks just like gold,' he thought. He took a step closer. 'But it really is gold! I've never seen anything like this before! How I would like to have some of that hair!' Greedily he stretched out his hands to pull some out. But the princess already knew what the boy was planning to do

and she immediately thought of a trick. She said:

'Will you help me, west wind,
Of all the winds the best?
Come and help me, west wind,
And drive away this pest.
Make him pant and make him puff,
Make him clutch the air—
For a little while will be enough
To let me comb my hair.'

When she had finished speaking, a gust of wind blew off Kurt's hat and dropped it down across the meadow.

Greedily Kurt stretched out his hands to pull out some of the princess's hair.

Kurt rushed off after his hat, but just when he was about to grab it, the wind blew it a little further away.

By the time Kurt had managed to get hold of his hat, the princess had finished combing her hair and she had put her hat back on. Kurt was out of breath from so much running. Angrily he glared at the princess.

'I'll get even with you tomorrow,' he growled. 'Just you wait!'

Just when Kurt was about to grab his hat, the wind blew it farther away.

184

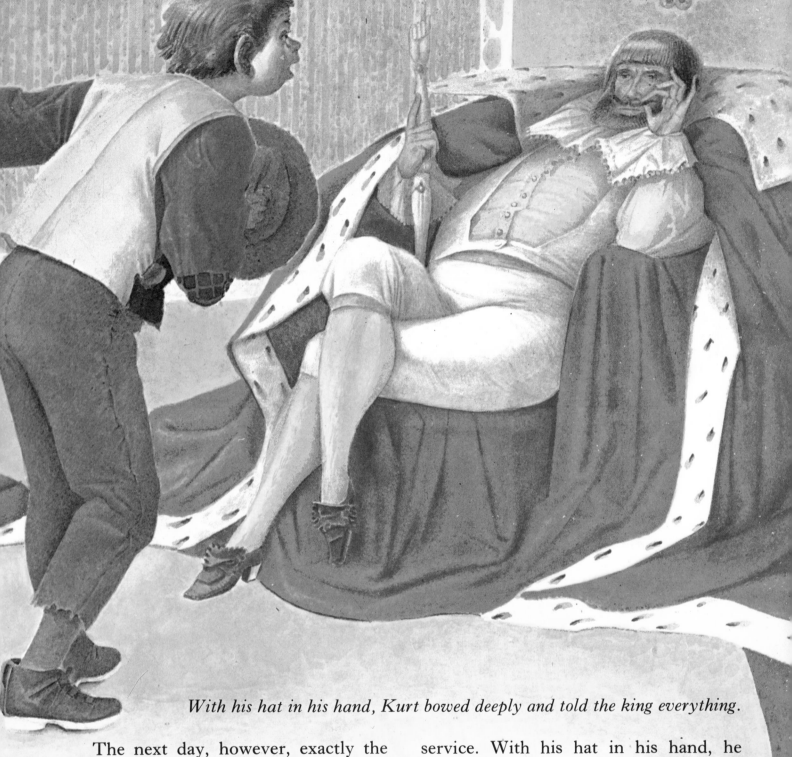

With his hat in his hand, Kurt bowed deeply and told the king everything.

The next day, however, exactly the same thing happened. The princess sat down in the grass to comb her hair. Greedy as ever, Kurt came closer. The princess called to the wind to help her and the next moment Kurt was chasing after his hat again.

The boy decided it was time to go and tell the king about the extraordinary goosegirl who had been taken into his

service. With his hat in his hand, he bowed deeply and told the king everything.

The king listened carefully, stroking his moustache.

'What you have just told me is indeed extraordinary,' the king said. 'And now you mention it, I don't think she looks like an ordinary girl either. I shall have to look into the matter.'

So the next day the king stole quietly

The king saw how a sudden gust of wind tore off Kurt's hat.

after the goosegirl to the meadow. He heard how she talked to the horse's head. Then he watched and saw how a sudden gust of wind tore off Kurt's hat, and he saw too that the girl's hair was of purest gold.

'The boy is right,' the king murmured. 'This goosegirl must be someone quite out of the ordinary.'

At the end of the day the king sent for the goosegirl.

'Tell me girl,' said the king in a kindly voice. 'Who are you? Who are your parents and where do you come from?'

The goosegirl curtsied low and said, 'Sire, I would greatly like to answer your questions, but I cannot. It would cost me my life if I did. No living soul must know who I am and where I come from.' There were tears in the princess's eyes.

'I can see that you would dearly like to pour your heart out to someone,' said the king. 'If you cannot tell your story to a living soul, why not tell it to . . . to the fireplace? You could do that, couldn't you?'

'Tell me girl,' said the king.
'Who are you?'

So that was what the girl did. She was happy now that she could pour out the whole story, even to the fireplace. She told it that she was the real princess and that the bride who was dancing in the banqueting hall was an impostor. And there was a great deal more she told the fireplace. She did not know that the king had gone up to the roof-garden, where he could put his ear against the chimney and hear everything that the princess was saying down below.

When the king had heard everything he ran quickly downstairs again. He took

A magnificent feast was held . . .

the real princess by the arm and led her into the banqueting hall.

The maid uttered a cry of terror when she saw the real princess come in with the king. She fled from the palace and no one ever saw her again.

The prince was overjoyed when he saw his true bride. She was even more beautiful than he had imagined. A magnificent feast was held that evening. Huge dishes loaded with delicious food were brought in. And—after sending their happy news to the princess's mother, the bridal pair danced long into the night.

THE LITTLE MERMAID

Once upon a time there was a beautiful little mermaid who lived with her father and her five sisters at the bottom of the sea.

Now you must not imagine that it was black and frightening in the ocean's depth. It was just the opposite. The little mermaid was the daughter of the Mer-king, and the palace in which she grew up was a splendid one. It was built of red and white coral, and through its many windows little fishes, some a delicate pale green and others a bright red and blue, would swim in and out. They were as much at home in the palace as they were among the rocks and the dark sea caves.

In the gardens surrounding the Mer-king's palace were the most gorgeous sea plants and trailing flowers which were a joy to gaze upon. The little mermaid loved the flowers especially, and she and her five sisters had gardens of their own which they decorated with glowing pebbles and all manner of entrancing colourful sea shells.

The mermaids had no mother, but they did have a grandmother—a handsome old Mer-lady whose tender care for her grandchildren was rewarded by their love.

The royal grandmother ruled the palace with a firm but kindly hand. And the Mer-king considered her so important that he granted her one of the highest honours. She, alone, was allowed to decorate her tail with oyster shells!

All the Mer-princesses were extremely beautiful, but the little mermaid, who was the youngest, had the prettiest hair—it was golden rather than reddish-brown—and the bluest eyes.

The grandmother cared for the little mermaid more than her sisters. This was not because she was prettier but because she was so quiet and gentle. And, it must be admitted, because she was so eager to hear the old lady's stories!

Day after day the little mermaid would beg her grandmother to tell her of the world above the sea.

'You say they do not have tails like ours!' she would remark in her soft, gentle voice. 'How very strange that seems! Oh, how I long to see these human beings for myself.'

And then her grandmother would tell her, as she had told her many times before, that she would not be permitted to leave the coral palace and swim freely in the blue sea until she was fifteen years old.

'Be patient, child,' the old lady would say kindly. 'Your time will come!'

But the little mermaid found it hard to be patient. She thought so much about the strange beings who lived above the sea that she even neglected her garden.

Then one day her sisters gave her a present for her garden and from that moment onwards the little mermaid spent all her free time there.

Their present was a strange one. It was a beautiful white marble statue of a young boy. It had come from a ship, wrecked at sea not far from their palace, and the five sisters had brought it home.

Day after day the youngest princess sat in her garden, staring at the statue and dreaming of the day when she would be old enough to find out for herself what real men and women would be like.

'How much longer must I wait?' she

Day after day the princess sat in her garden staring at the statue.

'Soon you will be fifteen,' said her grandmother.

asked her grandmother one morning as she set out to visit the statue. 'All my sisters have now been allowed to go above the sea—I am the only one who doesn't know what it is like.'

'The Mer-king's law cannot be broken,' said her grandmother patiently. 'You have not much longer to wait, for soon you will be fifteen.'

The little mermaid sighed as she sat down beside her grandmother. It was so hard to be patient!

'Ask your sisters to tell you again of the wonders they have seen above our blue sea,' the old lady said at last, after a long silence. 'Do not spend so much of your time dreaming in front of that boy-statue they gave you. Try and be more like them! They are always so gay . . .'

'You are right,' said the little princess. 'I will seek them out and ask them to talk to me of the other world.'

That day the little mermaid did not visit her garden. She went searching for her sisters. And when she found them she begged them to tell her all they had seen when they left home.

'So our little sister has time for us at last,' teased the eldest. 'Let me tell you what I did when I rose above the sea. I sat upon a sandbank in the moonlight and watched what happened in the town built along the shore. I saw men—they walked on two legs just like our grandmother said they would—and I saw many dull grey houses and high church towers from which came the sound of bells.'

'Is that all?' asked the little mermaid. 'Oh—not all,' said her eldest sister. 'But here is much nicer, I promise you.'

'Now tell me what you saw!' the little mermaid exclaimed, turning to the next of her sisters.

'But I did tell you!' protested her sister. 'Perhaps you were too young to listen properly. Well, when I rose to the surface of the sea, the sun was just setting, and the sky was so very beautiful that I could scarcely take my eyes away from it. Then I saw a flock of white swans and they too were beautiful—as beautiful as any of our fishes.'

'Was there more?' asked the little mermaid.

'I don't think so,' said her sister. 'I was quite tired when I came back but it was all great fun, you know.'

'I remember I swam into a bay where some children were playing,' said the third sister. 'I heard the birds singing in the wood which fringed the bay. But it was the children I liked.'

'What happened? Did you try to speak to them?' the little mermaid asked with an eager smile for she was thinking of her boy-statue.

'I wanted to play with them,' said her sister, 'as they swam about in the sea. But I must have frightened them, for they all swam away from me as fast as they could.'

'Well, I didn't see any humans,' said the fourth sister. 'I didn't venture very far. I just saw some fine sailing ships and some pretty sea gulls in the sky. If you ask me, it is much nicer under the sea with all our friends.'

'I don't agree with you,' said the fifth sister. 'When I went to the surface, it was winter. I saw giant icebergs chasing men in ships. It was very exciting and I sat on one of the icebergs until the night-clouds covered the sky.'

'I shall be fifteen in the spring,' said the little mermaid. 'I won't see any giant icebergs.'

'You will be free to go to the surface any time you choose once you are fifteen,' her eldest sister said.

That evening the five sisters, because they had talked so much about the world above, joined hands and rose to the surface, singing sweet, haunting songs as they circled the ships.

Left alone in the palace, the youngest mermaid was ready to weep, so much did she long to be with them. But mermaids

She swam upwards until she found herself rising out of a sea that was as smooth as glass.

cannot shed tears, and so she remained dry-eyed and miserable, waiting for their return.

Slowly the time passed, and then one day it was her birthday and she was fifteen years old! Her grandmother put a garland of white sea flowers on her head as a token of her new rank.

'Do not be disappointed if the world above us is not as beautiful as you wished it to be,' said the old lady.

'I won't,' promised the little mermaid, trembling with excitement. And she swam upwards until she found herself rising out of a sea that was as smooth as glass.

The little mermaid's blue eyes shone with pleasure as she looked up and saw above her the night sky lit by a hundred twinkling stars. And she thought, 'My dream of the world is coming true. This is the sky they see. My sisters said the sky was beautiful but they did not tell me about the stars.'

Then she saw, some distance away, a great ship lying at anchor, with only one white sail unfurled. Sailors were moving about the deck, and there was the sound of music and men's laughter.

The little mermaid swam nearer to the great ship. She went so close that she could peer into one of its lighted cabins and there she saw a tall, elegant young man. He was richly dressed and there was a golden crown embroidered on his robe.

'He must be a prince,' she said to herself. 'Only a prince would have such a noble bearing!'

It was growing late, but the little mermaid could not bear to leave the ship or cease watching the handsome prince. But then the sea, which a moment before had been so smooth and friendly, became suddenly fiercely angry.

The little mermaid knew and understood the sea and was not afraid. She saw its huge, raging waves strike the ship's side and sweep over her decks.

She heard the shouts of the sailors, who were not prepared for the storm, and she swam away from the stricken vessel.

But she could not bear to leave the prince, and so she waited to see how the royal ship would weather the tempest.

The ship struggled bravely against the battering waves for a time and the little mermaid began to hope that the skill of the sailors would save her.

Then, as the wind reached gale force, the sea surged in and the men let out a desperate cry of fear. It was just as if a giant hand had taken hold of their beautiful ship and was forcing her over on her side. She listed dangerously, and then began to sink.

In their terror the men aboard her jumped into the raging sea and the little mermaid searched for her prince among the drowning crew.

She saw him at last and she saw how weakly he was swimming.

'He will sink to the ocean's bed,' she thought, 'and then he will be mine for ever!'

Suddenly something her grandmother had told her made her terribly afraid for the young man. She had said that if a human fell into the sea and could not swim he would be lost for ever.

'I must save him,' the little mermaid

The little mermaid held the prince in her arms.

told herself. And she swam quickly to him, cradling his head in her arms, as she pulled him away from the wreck.

For the rest of that night the little mermaid held the prince in her arms. His eyes were closed and he scarcely seemed to breathe, but she stroked his face and kissed his hair as she kept him above the water. And the current drew them steadily towards land.

By morning the storm had passed, and the sea was calm and friendly again. But it had claimed the ship and the crew for there was no sign of them.

The loss of the beautiful ship did not concern the little mermaid; she had

She swam with him to the shore.

thoughts only for the prince. When she saw that they were now in some kind of deep bay she knew she had saved him.

She swam with him to the shore and laid him gently on the warm, firm sand. And she kissed him once again and begged him to open his eyes and speak to her.

But the prince did not open his eyes or make any sign that he was alive and the little mermaid grew afraid for him and wished that some other humans would come and help to save him.

Presently, from the little white chapel, which stood beyond the fringe of trees, came the sound of a bell ringing, and a

One of the girls saw the young man lying on the sand.

group of pretty young girls came out of the little church.

One of them saw the young man lying on the sand and as she ran towards him the little mermaid, terror-stricken in case she was seen, hid behind a large rock.

She watched, wide-eyed, as the girl stared down at the prince for a startled moment and then shouted to her friends to come and help her.

The little mermaid sighed with relief as the girl, with the aid of her friends, carried the young prince to their house.

As they passed the rock where she lay hidden, the prince opened his eyes for an instant and smiled.

'He thinks it is they who saved his life,' the little mermaid told herself mournfully. 'But what does that matter? He is alive!' And she made her way to the water's edge and plunged into the sea. She had been away from home for many hours and her grandmother, especially, would be growing anxious about her.

The little mermaid had always been quiet and thoughtful, but now she grew so quiet and showed so clearly that her joy was to sit before the marble boy-statue that her grandmother and her sisters were concerned for her.

'Why does she refuse to tell us what she saw when she visited the world above?' one of the sisters asked her grandmother.

'You must ask her,' said the wise old lady. 'If you ask her directly she will tell you.'

So the eldest of the sisters asked the little mermaid to confide in her.

'The statue reminds me of a prince I saved from the sea's fury,' said the little mermaid, with a heavy sigh. 'I think of him all the time, but I do not know where he lives . . .'

'But I know!' cried the eldest sister, pleased to be of help. 'We heard stories of the wreck and how the prince aboard her was found on the golden sands of the bay. Come, I know where his palace stands. It is large and yellow with steps running straight down to the sea.'

'Will you take me to it now?' asked the little mermaid, suddenly alive with excitement and eagerness.

'Of course,' said her sister, and she took the little mermaid by the hand and swam with her until it was time to rise out of the water. There in front of them was the palace.

She was so full of joy at having found where her beloved lived.

The little mermaid left her sister and rested for a moment on the marble steps. She was so full of joy at having found where her beloved prince lived that she could not speak. It was enough to gaze up at the fine palace and think about him, and wish him happiness.

After that first visit the little mermaid went many times to the golden palace. Sometimes, on bright moonlit nights, when the prince thought he was alone, the little mermaid stole up quite close to him as he sat on the sea wall.

At other times she watched him from a distance as he sailed his boat or dived from the high rocks.

There were days and nights when the prince did not appear and the little mermaid became sad and downcast. And then her sisters would try to make her smile as they told her stories they had overhead from the fishermen. These were stories about the prince—how brave he was, how kind and thoughtful he was at home, and how all his subjects loved him dearly.

'Does a human have to die?' the mermaid asked her grandmother one day.

'Yes,' came the reply. 'We go on living for three hundred years and then we become foam on the sea. Human beings have souls which go on living for ever—even though their bodies die and turn to dust. But then they live only a short time compared to us.'

'I wish I could be a human being,' sighed the little mermaid, thinking of her prince.

'That is a foolish wish,' said the grand old lady sharply. 'If it came true you would not have a soul unless you found a human man who loved you with all his heart. Then it is possible you might be given a part of his soul.'

The little mermaid sighed again as she said, 'Humans walk on two funny things they call legs. Could they possibly love us Mer-people who only have long scaly tails?'

'Of course not!' exclaimed her grandmother. 'But our long scaly tails are much more beautiful than legs . . .'

The little mermaid thought much about what her grandmother had said and she began to long to have legs like her prince.

At last she made up her mind to pay a visit to the sea-witch, whose home was by a deep, dark whirlpool far away from the red and white coral palace and beautiful gardens. To reach it she must pass through dreadful black, slimy swamps where the sea-witch kept her serpents and monster toads.

It was a truly terrifying journey and when at last the little mermaid stood before the old witch she was still trembling.

'Help me mother-witch,' she began in a weak, frightened voice. 'Help me to gain my heart's desire. I want to rid myself of my tail and have in its place two legs, the kind humans use for walking.'

'I know the reason for this foolish wish,' said the old sea-witch with a shrill, cruel laugh. 'You have fallen in love with a prince. You want him to love you and share his immortal soul with you.'

'Yes, that is true,' the princess admitted.

'Are you prepared to endure the most terrible suffering?' the witch demanded, as she stirred the bubbling mixture in her

The witch filled her kettle-spoon with the potion and held it out to her.

cauldron. 'Are you ready to turn to foam if you fail to win the prince's love?'

'I am ready,' whispered the mermaid.

And the witch filled her kettle-spoon with some of the steaming potion and held it out to the princess. 'Three drops of this will change your tail to the props men call legs,' she told her.

'But I must not drink it now, the little mermaid protested. 'I must first swim to his palace.'

'I will pour the magic potion into a phial,' said the sea-witch. 'Drink it when you reach the palace. And now I will take your sweet voice in payment.'

And she cut out the little mermaid's tongue, leaving her dumb and speechless. Then she gave her the phial and with a cruel smile sent her on her way.

The sun had not yet risen when the little mermaid arrived at the prince's palace. She pulled herself out of the water and over the sea wall. Then she sipped the magic liquid in the phial.

Pain as keen as the sharpest knife pierced the little mermaid's body, and she lay down at the foot of the marble steps and closed her eyes.

How long she lay there she did not know, but when at last she stirred it was to find the young prince kneeling at her side. Covering her with his cloak, he began asking her who she was and how she came to be lying there.

'Never have I seen a maid so lovely!' the prince declared, and he put out a gentle hand to stroke the little mermaid's long golden hair.

The little mermaid gazed up at him, speechless, and her blue eyes were so bright and loving that the young man was suddenly at a loss for words.

'Did you come from the sea?' he asked finally. 'Was some ship perhaps wrecked on the rocks?'

And when the girl still did not answer, the prince helped her to rise. As she stood, slim and straight on her two legs, it was as if she were standing on nails. How right the witch had been! The pain was dreadful, but the little mermaid gave no sign of her suffering.

The prince showed his surprise as the beautiful young girl moved towards the

She awoke to find the young prince kneeling at her side and covering her with his cloak.

marble steps. She moved with the grace of an angel and he stared at her, fascinated by her airy lightness. Then he hurried her into the palace where he called some of his mother's ladies-in-waiting to come to him.

'See that my guest has all the clothes she requires,' he ordered.

So the little mermaid was robed in rich dresses of silk and muslin and she was so delicately lovely and so clearly eager to please that she became a great favourite with the prince. But she could neither speak nor sing and this often made her sad.

She saw how the prince loved music and how the pretty court ladies were able to please him with their singing.

'Once I had the sweetest voice in the Mer-kingdom,' she thought sadly.

But then one day two of the most beautiful of the slave girls danced for their royal master. The little mermaid saw the pleasure on his face as he watched them and when they had gone, she rose to her feet and started to dance.

So light was she and so graceful that she was like thistledown blown this way and that by the softest of breezes. And the prince and all those watching were quite entranced by her movements.

The prince especially was completely enraptured, and when she ceased, he called out, 'More, more, my little one.'

Every step caused the little mermaid the most terrible suffering, but the pain was nothing compared to her joy at knowing she was pleasing her prince. And she began dancing again.

When the prince decided that she had danced long enough, he summoned her to his side, and began talking to her in a low, kindly voice.

'I want you always by my side,' he said. 'From now on you shall be my constant little companion and friend. When I go out riding, you shall come with me. When I retire at night you shall sleep on a velvet cushion in my own apartments.'

The mermaid's blue eyes glowed with love at this and she longed to tell the prince all that was in her heart. But she could only smile.

The next day she went riding with the prince, and he talked to her of the beauty of the woods and of the pleasure he had in listening to the sweet songs of the birds. And the little mermaid smiled and nodded, longing to hear him speak of the love he felt for herself.

But the young prince did not speak of love, only of friendship and of the joy he found at being in her company.

That night the little mermaid stole down to the water's edge. As she stood in the cool soothing water to ease her aching feet she thought of her father, the Merking, and of her grandmother and her five sisters.

'If only I could see them again,' she told herself. 'I would be able to make them understand why I had to leave them.'

One night, some weeks later, she did see her five sisters again. They rose out of the water and called a greeting to her, and the little mermaid told them about her love for the prince and how she could not leave him—not even though she missed her home and the love of her family.

'We will tell our father,' said the eldest. 'He mourns you as if you were already turned to foam. Have courage, little sister, we shall come when we can to speak with you and give you news.'

Soon after she had seen her sisters, the prince took her climbing and as they sat together on the highest peak of the mountain the little mermaid looked at the young man with questioning eyes. Was this the moment when at last he would tell her how much he had come to love her?

But the prince did not look upon his faithful companion as a possible bride. He thought of her only as his dear little sister. And so, without any idea of how much he was hurting her, he began to speak of the plans his parents had made to find him a suitable wife.

'They say they have already found me a beautiful princess,' he said lightly. 'By all accounts she has a sweet nature as well. But then we shall soon find out what she is really like for tomorrow we set sail for her kingdom. And you, of course, will accompany us.'

Early next morning the prince and his

party boarded the royal ship. And the little mermaid hid her suffering and smiled whenever the prince turned to her.

But that night, when the prince and his friends were sound asleep in their cabins, the little mermaid went on deck, and the silver moon shone down on her sad face as she thought of what would happen to her.

Then somewhere out at sea she heard the gentle, whispering voices of her five sisters. 'If the prince marries another,' the eldest called, 'we will go at once to the sea-witch and ask her help.'

The silver moon shone down on her sad face.

The meeting between the beautiful princess and the handsome young prince took place the next day, and only those with dull eyes and leaden hearts failed to note that, for these two young people, it was no less than love at first sight. And the prince proclaimed his intentions of marrying the princess on the morrow.

After the wedding the royal party made its merry way back to the ship and, as night fell, the little mermaid once again found herself alone on deck.

She was so sad at the thought of all she had lost that not even the voices of her sisters calling to her from the sea could rouse her. But then the eldest, rising up out of the waves, cried, 'We have been to the witch. She has taken our long hair in exchange for this knife. Kill the prince with it. If you do, you will save yourself.'

The mermaid accepted the knife. She found the prince asleep when she reached his cabin and in his dreams he spoke his bride's name. As she heard it, the little mermaid threw down the fatal knife and, rushing up on deck, plunged into the sea.

But she did not, as she expected, turn to foam. Almost at once she was caught up in the strong arms of the wind.

Far below she saw the prince come out on deck to search for her and she had time to blow him a warm, fragrant kiss before the wind carried her far away to a new home in the starry heavens.

Almost at once she was caught up in the strong arms of the wind.

208